ALL THIS FOR LOVE

Though cousins, Sally Browning and Philippa Frome are identical – in looks but not in character. When the spoilt Philippa persuades her identical 'twin' to pretend to be Mrs Frome so Philippa can run off on holiday with her secret love, Sally can only reluctantly agree. She embarks upon a new life of wealth and luxury, fooling all and sundry – even Philippa's invalid husband Martin. Soon accustomed to her new role and to the deceptions she is loath to make, Sally finds she has more devotion and love to give – especially to the ailing Martin – than she had dared to imagine.

ALL THIS FOR LOVE

All This For Love

by

Denise Robins

Dales Large Print Books
Long Preston, North Yorkshire,
BD23 4ND, England.

British Library Cataloguing in Publication Data.

Robins, Denise
    All this for love.

    A catalogue record of this book is
    available from the British Library

    ISBN   978-1-84262-530-9 pbk

First published in Great Britain in 1935 by Mills & Boon Ltd.

Copyright © 1935 by Denise Robins

Cover illustration © John Hancock by arrangement with
P.W.A. International Ltd.

MORAY DISTRICT COUNCIL DEPARTMENT OF LEISURE AND LIBRARIES

F 678756

Dales Large Print is an imprint of Library Magna Books Ltd.

Printed and bound in Great Britain by
T.J. (International) Ltd., Cornwall, PL28 8RW

For
Jane Lindsay

1935

1

It was with a slight feeling of nervousness that Sally Browning rang the bell at the big house in Harley Street which bore a brass plate with the inscription: *'Mr Martin Frome, M.D., F.R.C.S.'*

She was not at all sure that she would be a welcome visitor. She had not seen her cousin, Philippa, who was married to Martin Frome, for the last few years, and it was quite possible that Philippa had no interest in her these days, added to which the Frome household was under a cloud of misfortune at the moment, because a month ago, Martin, one of the most brilliant young surgeons of the day, had been the victim of a terrible motor smash.

This morning's paper had informed Sally that Martin Frome had just returned to his house from the nursing-home, and it was feared that he would be doomed to his bed for the rest of his life. The accident had caused an injury to the spine, and paralysis.

Sally had felt that she must come along and offer her sympathies even if she was not

11

allowed to see her cousin.

The butler opened the door, gave her a somewhat surprised look and said:

'Oh, madam, I'm so sorry, but I thought you were in, and when the master asked for you...'

Then he stopped and stared. Sally found her cheeks growing pink. Good heavens! He was mistaking her for Philippa. Was she still so like her? Of course she knew there had always been a marked resemblance between them. As children they had frequently been mistaken for twins. But surely, thought Sally, in her rather shabby suit and the little stone marten tie which had seen better days, she could not be so like the wealthy and beautifully gowned Mrs Frome as to deceive one of her own servants! However, apparently it was so. But now the butler had discovered his mistake. Sally smiled and murmured:

'I am Mrs Frome's cousin, Miss Browning.'

'Your pardon, miss,' said the butler as he stepped back. 'But it's the most astonishing resemblance.'

'Do you think Mrs Frome would see me?'

'If you'll just wait one moment, miss, I'll let the mistress know that you're here,' said the butler, took another astonished look at the slim young figure in blue, and showed her into a large dining-room.

Sally sat down. She felt suddenly depressed. The room was full of massive, handsome furniture. There was a cut-glass bowl of bronze chrysanthemums in the centre of the polished table, and neatly arranged piles of society journals. A typical doctor's waiting-room. But there would be no more patients waiting to see Martin Frome. The papers had said this morning that he would never recover. What a tragedy!

And then the door opened. The butler came back, and said:

'Will you come upstairs to madam's boudoir, please, miss.'

A moment later Sally found herself in that boudoir, quite the loveliest room she had ever seen, with its soft golden carpet and gold net curtains through which September sunlight filtered. Sally was almost dazed for a few moments by a riot of colour and luxury such as she had only seen on the films. Everywhere, that golden glow, over the painted furniture, the chaise-longue with its satin cushions, the roses and carnations, the books, and glittering array of expensive ornaments. Then she saw her cousin Philippa lying against rose and gold brocade, in a black chiffon rest suit – and Sally looked no further. It gave her a shock to see a face so like her own.

Philippa in her turn was staring … at first a little scornfully at the badly cut suit and a hat which screamed 'cheap sales' … then with amazement at Sally herself.

'Heavens!' exclaimed Philippa, sitting upright. 'I'd forgotten how alike we were. My *dear* Sally ... come here and take off your hat.'

Sally laughed with some embarrassment and advanced towards the chaise-longue, removing her hat as she did so.

'It's ages since we met, isn't it, Philippa? How are you? You know your butler thought I was you!'

'And no wonder...' said Philippa under her breath.

She continued to fix an intent and amazed gaze upon her cousin's face. Yes, they had been like twins as children. Queer, first cousins resembling each other so closely. Of course, Sally's hair wasn't done like her own in that fashionable way, caught in a bunch of curls at the back of her head, but it was of the same fairness, almost silver-gilt, and the eyes were the same, more grey than blue, widely set. They both had slightly tip-tilted noses and skins of delicate, transparent quality. Both were tanned, Sally naturally so, Philippa very much made up. Philippa's mouth in repose was hard. Sally's lips were sweetly curved and the whole expression of her face was kinder, but except for details the two girls were the counterpart of each other.

'I can't get over it,' said Philippa, and flung herself back on the cushions.

'It *is* odd,' agreed Sally, 'awfully odd to see

somebody so like oneself.'

'Disconcerting, too, my dear. I'm not sure that I like it. I rather prided myself upon being uniquely beautiful.'

The brazen conceit of that made Sally smile.

'Where have you sprung from?' Philippa questioned her.

'From South Africa,' said Sally.

'What on earth have you been doing there?'

'I'll tell you,' said Sally. 'But first of all … my father is dead.'

'Poor old Uncle Bob. And are you quite alone now?'

'Yes. But I'm engaged to be married.'

'Who to?'

Philippa was only faintly interested, but she was wondering whether, if Sally were properly dressed, the men she knew would fall for her. Of course it wasn't only face and figure that counted with a man. She, Philippa, attracted men because she was amusing as well as lovely. Sally didn't seem to be amusing. She had always been a quiet, staid little thing.

Sally explained her position. Until her twenty-first birthday she had lived with her father, a retired doctor, in a suburb of London, where she had spent a rather uneventful girlhood, marked by only one important and unhappy episode, the death of her mother. From that time onward she had kept house

15

for Dr Browning and found plenty to do, because there wasn't much money, and those who would lead an economic existence cannot lead a lazy one.

After Mrs Browning's death had come a happier time following upon Sally's introduction to Rex Trenchman, a young South African whom she had met at the local tennis club. Rex was in England on holiday. He was in a firm of accountants in Johannesburg. Before he returned to South Africa he had succumbed to the charms of fair-haired, grey-eyed Sally, and she had promised to marry him.

Philippa listened, passing a polishing pad over her red-lacquered nails. It was all news to her because it was so long since she had been in touch with this side of her family. Philippa's mother had been the late Dr Browning's only sister and the girls had seen a lot of each other as children. But Philippa's father had had money and so later on she had moved and lived in different circles from Sally. Sally had been asked to Philippa's wedding, which had been a grand affair in the West End, but she had had 'flu at the time and been unable to attend. Since then she had not received any invitations to Philippa's home in Harley Street. On one or two occasions she remembered showing a new portrait of Philippa to her father, remarking with a laugh, 'Little Sally might look like that in a Molyneux dress.'

The old doctor had replied:

'Yes, you and Philippa are physically as alike as two peas, but thank God you are not so in character. I hear that girl's her mother all over again, and she was a hard, selfish girl, poor Jenny. And you're like *your* mother, an angel, God bless her.'

Sally often smiled over those words. She wasn't really so keen on being an angel. She would like to have had some of Philippa's chances in life. But those chances only came when one was dressed by the world's leading designers and met people like Martin Frome. Not if one had to make one's own clothes and stay at home.

Last July, Sally told Philippa, Dr Browning insisted upon Sally taking a trip to South Africa, which was to be her future home. It was time, he said, that she met her prospective 'in-laws', especially as Rex intended to come back to London next spring and marry her.

Sally scarcely reached Johannesburg before a cable recalled her. The old man had suddenly been taken ill with angina, and he died while Sally was on the way back to him.

'How miserable for you!' said Philippa, and told herself that that last manicure had been rotten, and she would go somewhere else to-morrow.

'It hasn't been very happy,' agreed Sally. 'I

had to get rid of our little house ... you remember we lived in Purley ... and, of course, it's been very lonely and a bit difficult, because Daddy's left only about two pounds a week for me to live on.'

'Why not get married?' said Philippa.

Sally flushed and did not answer for a moment.

There was nothing she would have liked better than to have gone straight back to South Africa to Rex. She was very much in love with him. But there was a letter in her bag at this moment which she had received from him which crushed those hopes.

'I don't know that it's wise for you to come back to South Africa just yet, darling,' one of the paragraphs had told her. 'It's frightfully difficult for a girl to get a job here at the moment, and you might fix a better one in London. I hope this time next year that we shall be able to get married.'

Sally had brooded over those words. It was so depressing to think that her marriage was still such a long way off. Lengthy engagements were not good things. It seemed to her best that lovers should marry in the 'first fine careless rapture' of their love.

And she would like Rex to have wanted her so madly that he could not bear to live apart from her. She, herself, was impulsive, passionate, perhaps a little too intense, she told herself with a wry smile. Rex was so sensible and level-headed. He saw the practical side of things.

'It *is* disappointing, isn't it, Philippa?' she asked her cousin.

'Very,' said Philippa, and yawned.

'I shall try and get a job in London to augment my two pounds a week,' smiled Sally.

Philippa was vaguely sympathetic. Two pounds wouldn't have paid a week's taxi fares for her. Then they talked of Martin.

'I've been having a *ghastly* time!' said Philippa.

'I'm sure you have. And how awful for him, after leading that busy, wonderful life, and loving his work … to be tied to his couch … oh, how dreadful! Isn't a cure at all likely, Philippa?'

'They don't think so,' said Philippa gloomily. 'He may walk again in time, but the injury to his spine has caused paralysis, and at the moment it seems to be hopeless.'

'It must be marvellous for him to have you,' said Sally. 'And a wonderful thing for you to know that you can help him bear it.'

Philippa relapsed into silence. She felt suddenly savagely angry. God! Did her fool of a cousin really imagine that she found it 'wonderful' to have to sit for hours beside a sick-bed and be chained to that job for the rest of her life?

She, too, had been brooding over a certain paragraph in a letter which had come this morning. A letter of very different significance to the one which Sally had received from her fiancé. It had said:

'And I love you … I love you. *I love you.* You know it. You knew it last night when I held you in my arms. Darling, you drive me crazy. I suppose I'm a cad when poor old Frome is done for. But, you beautiful thing, you can't be allowed to spend the rest of your life being a nurse! The damnable thing is that I haven't a cent, so I can't take you away. What the hell are we going to do…'

Whenever Philippa recalled that paragraph she ran long slender fingers through her fair curls and gave little moaning sighs.

'Ivor! Ivor!'

Ivor Lexon was a handsome, attractive, and altogether useless member of society who spent most of his time going from one cocktail party to another, sponging on people with fuller pockets than his own, wriggling out of debts as easily as he slid into them.

He was supposed to be on the Stock Exchange, but he never did any work. What income he possessed came from an old aunt to whom he showed his gratitude by saying an almost daily prayer that she would speedily depart this life and leave him everything.

Women were fascinated by Ivor. Nobody could be so amusing at a party. He played the piano, he danced, he made love with a grace that induced the opposite sex to forgive him his many failings. Philippa Frome would not even admit the failings. It had been in her company that he had lately spent most of his leisure. Everybody knew that they were having an affair. That is, everybody but Philippa's husband.

Philippa knew quite well that Martin had no use for men of Ivor's type, but he had always been too generous to begrudge his young wife any amusement she wanted. He knew that he had to neglect her occasionally because of his work, and if she wanted Ivor Lexon to take her out, why not? Martin trusted Philippa.

They had only been married three years. At first Philippa had been thrilled by his charming personality and his brains. She, who had been spoilt all her life, thought it would be amusing to be the wife of an eminent surgeon in such a big position. But soon after their honeymoon she had grown bored. Martin was always out, operating. At hospitals, nursing-homes, consultations. That was his life, his work. And she was resentful because he was too tired to frivol or dance until the dawn, which she adored to do.

Now, of course, things were a thousand

times worse. She could not bear sickness in any form. She had tried her best, she argued to herself, while she lay there this afternoon with her lover's passionate letter crushed against her breast. She had tried … but she couldn't bear that grim, supine figure which had once been the alert and vigorous form of the man she had married. It just made her shudder when she touched him. She was mean, weak, despicable, all the things people liked to say, but she could not anticipate the rest of life tied to Martin as he was now, a helpless wreck. His eyes, so alive, so intense in his thin face, followed her wherever she went, were hungry for her, demanding like his voice. Ever since his smash he had kept on saying:

'Phil … come and sit by me, Phil…' Or:

'Phil, the pain doesn't seem so bad when you're with me… I want you, Phil…'

And she didn't want him. She was in love, in love with Ivor.

That was the trouble. Ivor couldn't afford to take her away, even if she chose to behave badly enough to desert Martin now when he was most in need of her. Her creature comforts meant too much. She couldn't give up the life she lead as Mrs Martin Frome, her allowance, her sports car, her lovely clothes. She didn't love Ivor as much as all that. She would never love anybody more than herself.

But she loved him in her way. And oh, she

was bored, bored with this ministering angel business.

'So marvellous for you to be able to help Martin...' Sally was saying.

Philippa looked resentfully at her through languorous, silken lashes.

Perhaps Sally had that sort of nature. A pity she couldn't take on the job if she thought that it would be so marvellous.

With that thought came others. Suddenly Philippa found herself in a whirling sea of thought, of fantastic ideas, flights of imagination in which she disappeared from this house of gloom and was wafted somewhere into space with Ivor who meant glowing, passionate life, while Sally sat by that couch downstairs in the library, the ministering angel in her place.

Wild thoughts, of course. But they interested Philippa intensely. When Sally asked if she was boring her, Philippa answered feverishly:

'No, you mustn't go, Sally. I want to talk to you.'

Somebody knocked on the door.

'What is it?' Philippa called irritably.

A maid answered:

'Please, madam, Watson says the master would like you to go down to him if you are rested.'

'Tell him I can't come for a few minutes,' said Philippa sharply.

And Sally thought:

'I can't imagine myself not flying down to him ... if he were Rex lying there, calling for me.'

And there followed upon this thought another rather terrifying one:

'Does marriage change all that ... doesn't one stay in love ... does it all become a nuisance...?'

But no, she wasn't going to let it be like that when she married Rex ... she would go on feeling as she did now, that it was like death to be parted from him. Once again the memory of his letter hit Sally rather like a blow across the face. *He* could bear to be separated from *her* for a whole year. And yet he loved her. Well, people were different. Perhaps Philippa loved her husband, but was cool and practical about it, like Rex. Perhaps it wouldn't do for everybody to be as full of warm impulses, as intense as she was herself.

Philippa was talking to her earnestly now.

She wanted to know everything about Sally. There was so little to know that it was soon told. Philippa learned all the details about Sally's engagement, the present depressing position and the inadvisability of her returning at once to Johannesburg on the off chance of getting work.

Philippa looked at her with eyes grown hard ... very different eyes from Sally's when they had that flint-like expression.

'You're lucky,' she said. 'Lucky to be free for a year, my dear.'

'I don't think so. I want to get back to Rex.'

'We're none of us satisfied,' said Philippa with a short laugh.

'But aren't you...' began Sally, then flushed, and added: 'I suppose now, of course, you can't be. It's tragic for you having Martin so ill...'

'Tragic isn't the word. My life simply isn't worth living.'

'But why?' came from Sally, shocked and wide-eyed.

Philippa stood up, moved restlessly to the window, found a cigarette, lit it, and began to walk up and down the big golden room on bare feet with restless steps. Rather like a panther, Sally thought.

Philippa, brows knit, said:

'Of course you wouldn't understand, but you see, I ... I'm not in love with my husband any more. There, that's the truth and you might as well know it.'

'I see,' said Sally. 'But how ... dreadful.'

'My dear child, you weren't born yesterday. You know that these things happen.'

'Yes, I know. But I always thought you and Martin were so happy.'

'We were, but we were never really suited.'

'And does he feel the same?'

'No ... that's the worst part of it. He

doesn't. He's still madly in love with me.'

'That *is* dreadful,' said Sally.

Philippa turned to her with a swift movement. Her small white teeth snapped together.

'It's worse than you can imagine, living with a man who's in love with you when you don't love him any more. And under the present circumstances, it's hell.'

'Of course, I see. He needs you more than ever now that he's lost everything else.'

'Oh, I know you'll be horrified … but we haven't the same natures, Sally. I can't do this "good angel" business for long. It drives me crazy.'

Sally sat silent a moment, fingering her stone marten tie. She felt a queer little shudder run through her. Her cousin's personality was overpowering … passionate … yes, they were both passionate people, but in different ways. Philippa was concentrated upon herself and only herself. She couldn't make sacrifices … not even for that unfortunate man downstairs who must be going through a little hell of his own.

Sally felt that the atmosphere of the golden luxurious bedroom was becoming almost stifling. Coupled with faint contempt of this supreme egotist, was immense pity for Martin. She knew nothing much about him except the things she had heard from others but she could pity him, oh yes! For what had life left to him, having taken away his health and the love of this wife whom he adored?

Impetuously Sally said:

'He must never know…'

Philippa stared.

'You mean Martin must never know that I don't love him any more?'

'Yes. Because if he did, what would he have left?'

Philippa narrowed her eyes.

'It's a question of one or the other of us having nothing left. Perhaps I feel *I* can't go on.'

A sick look came into Sally's eyes.

'There isn't … someone else?'

Caution overcame Philippa's desire to talk about Ivor. Sally was a little prude. Or anyhow, her principles were too high to allow her to condone the love affair of a married woman. Better not talk about Ivor. She said:

'No, it isn't that. It's just that I want to get away. This house is like a prison to me, and Martin a gaoler.'

Now Sally felt faintly sorry for her.

'My dear, isn't it just that you need a holiday? Your nerves are all to pieces. Martin's dreadful accident has upset you.'

'Perhaps I *do* need a *long* holiday.'

'Then why not take it?'

'Because I can't get away. It isn't that Martin actually keeps me at his side, but that is what is demanded of me. His relations … his friends … the doctor … all of them would think me a cad if I went away now for any length of time. He doesn't seem to want anybody near him but me, and when I'm not there there's only his male nurse, Watson, who carries him round. Oh, I tell you, Sally, it's driving me mad!'

Sally looked at her a trifle helplessly.

'I wish I could do something. If there was anything…'

'Perhaps there is!' said Philippa in a breathless voice, and came and sat beside her and gripped Sally's wrist. 'You say you want a job … that you're hard up … well, why not take a month here in this house *in my place?*'

Sally stared, then her cheeks burned with colour and she drew away from Philippa, laughing.

'My dear Phil … don't be mad!'

'Why is it so mad? You're exactly like me… I've only got to have your hair curled like mine and put some of my things on you and I swear nobody would tell the difference. Didn't the butler mistake you for me, even in your own clothes? I was in Le Touquet just before Martin's accident and got sunburned. You're brown from Africa. We're both terribly alike at the moment. I swear even Martin would be deceived…'

'I don't believe it. Why, your own husband…'

'My dear, it isn't as though he'd make a

critical examination or *look* for differences. Since his accident his head has been bad and he never has strong lights. His eyes hurt ... the library is kept dim and so is his bedroom, and until he gets better he won't be allowed very strong lights. This injury to the spine has affected his eyes in some way – not dangerously. They're hoping to cure it. They're hoping to cure *him* in time. But God knows how long that will take. Months – years! Anyhow, he'd never notice it if you just did the things that I do.'

Philippa broke off, breathing hard and fast.

'You'd enjoy being the good angel, wouldn't you?' she added. 'I'm sure it's in your line. You'd read to him, talk to him, play gramophone records to him. He's crazy about music. It would be so simple. It isn't as though Martin and I were living together as husband and wife at the moment. It's just a question of a patient and his nurse.'

Sally listened to all this in bewildered fashion. Philippa's meaning was clear enough, but Sally just could not consider it seriously. It was the craziest thing she had ever heard.

'Even if I consented to do it, the thing would fail from the first half-hour,' she said. 'There'd be some sort of slip... I'd say something or I wouldn't know something that he was talking about ... or he'd see a difference *some*where.'

'I tell you he wouldn't. We have the same timbre of voices. He would never notice differences of details such as tricks of mannerism, etc. And we could have a long, long talk and I'd coach you … tell you all that I've been doing … write you a list of all the people we know. Sally, we used to act together when we were children. Don't you remember what fun it was when we took each other's parts and deceived Uncle Bob and Aunt Grace? And even my own people… Why shouldn't we do it now?'

'Because I think the whole idea is preposterous and I can't believe you mean it.'

'But I do!'

And Philippa continued to state a hundred reasons why Sally should consent … why the plan would work … why the deception would never be discovered. At the back of her brain was the mad, pulsating thought that if she could slip out of this house *as Sally,* she could go to Ivor. She could have money… Sally could get it from Martin and send it to her … she and Ivor could have a marvellous, wonderful time somewhere together where nobody would find them. Later, of course, she would have to come back. But it would be a few weeks of life worth living for … worth remembering … it would be a holiday she would not dare take unless Sally were left behind to masquerade as Martin's wife. Then it would be quite safe

... no questions would be asked ... and Martin would never know, never suffer.

Philippa knew perfectly well that she dared not let Sally even guess about Ivor, otherwise she would never consent to such a thing, so she harped on the fact that she needed a complete holiday and that it would be cruel to leave Martin alone.

'You could do it, Sally, say for just one month. From now till the first of October. You'd have a marvellous time apart from the ministrations to Martin. You've never led this sort of life, and it would be fun for you to live here, wear my lovely clothes, have a car, a chauffeur to drive you about, all the parties you'd get asked to, as me. And of course I'd see that you got a job when I came back ... as secretary or something ... and you could save up for your wedding.'

Sally could hardly speak. At first she had laughed at the idea and thought Philippa crazy. But now she could see that her cousin was in deadly earnest. With all these arguments and pleadings hurled at her head, she began to feel as though a net was being drawn round her. Almost against her will she was listening ... wondering if such a hare-brained scheme were possible.

What would Rex think of it? Of course he would be furious if she masqueraded for a month as Mrs Martin Frome ... even if it did only mean her sitting beside a sick man's couch. She told Philippa so.

'Don't be absurd!' said Philippa. 'What could he possibly object to? You won't be implicated. Nobody will ever know that you were not me. You can just tell your fiancé that you have got a job as my secretary. Ask him to write to you here, care of me.'

Sally felt quite hot and weak. She shook her head at her cousin.

'Honestly, Phil dear, it's absurd.'

But Philippa Frome was used to getting her own way, and having formed this idea she refused to relinquish it. She was fighting for more than Sally knew ... fighting for one glorious month with Ivor.

She began to argue and plead all over again. She enlarged on her own nervous, unhappy condition and the terrible necessity for a holiday without Martin being left to suffer. She assured Sally that she would be an angel from heaven if she would do this thing. An angel to Martin as well. Martin needed someone who would be tender and gentle and patient, and Sally could supply all these needs.

Of all the arguments that one appealed to Sally most. She did feel so sorry for Martin.

'But even if I consented, Philippa,' at length she said feebly, 'I'm sure I'd give the whole show away, and then...'

'Oh then,' broke in Philippa impatiently, 'we'd just say we did it for a joke.'

'It's dangerous.'

'But rather thrilling ... don't you think it would be rather thrilling?' said Philippa.

'I don't know.'

'Well, will you make the first move ... will you just give it a trial, now, this moment?'

'This moment!' repeated Sally, aghast.

'Yes, nobody knows you're here except Denham, our butler, and he won't give you away if I say a few words to him, because he adores Martin and was butler to Martin's father before him. Let me do your hair quickly and put you into one of my dresses, then go down to the library and speak to Martin and see what happens and come back and tell me.'

Sally shook her head.

'I couldn't.'

'Sally, I beg you...' Philippa's eyes were actually full of tears. She seemed at breaking point. 'I swear if you don't help me out of this, there'll be an awful disaster ... I shall just run away and leave Martin. I must get away and nobody in the world but you can help me.'

More arguments, more pleading, then tears. Philippa clinging to Sally, beseeching her. And Sally, always too warm-hearted, too generous, hating to witness other people's griefs, found herself consenting to give the maddest scheme that had ever been conceived, a trial.

2

Outside the door of the library in the house of Martin Frome, M.D., F.R.C.S., Sally Browning stood dressed as any woman would like to imagine herself, in a Molyneux afternoon toilette of some exquisite blue and grey flowered chiffon, and a big straw hat with a charming 'floppy' brim on the side of her head. Her lips had been reddened and her lashes darkened and her face had seemed, veritably, the face of Philippa when she had looked amazedly at herself in a mirror before she left that bedroom upstairs.

'You *are* me,' Philippa had told her with a hysterical laugh. 'Just as I appeared at Goodwood. And now you can tell Martin that you're going to Lady Gordon-Bingham's garden party and that you only have a few minutes to spare him... I'll bet you a thousand pounds that he won't see through it.'

Sally, outside the library door, was in such an agony of nerves and fright that she was shaking. It was quite crazy ... and yet, if the scheme worked ... well, why shouldn't she be Martin Frome's ministering angel for a month and why shouldn't the unhappy Philippa go away? Certainly it was a novel job … but she, Sally, would be doing two people a kindness and she could certainly not be bored by it.

Eleven years ago, when she and Philippa had been little girls of thirteen, they had done this sort of thing. Yes, they had fooled their own parents … and it had been a thrill. Wasn't some of the old thrill returning now?

Sally drew a deep breath, and clutched the beautiful embroidered bag and a pair of long suède gloves more tightly in her hot little fingers.

'Well, here goes,' she said to herself. 'You said you'd do this crazy thing, Sally Browning, so go ahead!'

She opened the library door.

At first she could see nothing but shadows in the big dim room. The blinds were drawn. The sun was not allowed to enter here. Row upon row of leather-bound books looked strangely gloomy and forbidding on their shelves. And on a sofa at right angles to the big carved fireplace lay a man against a pile of cushions. Very still he lay … big body outlined under a soft Jaeger rug which was thrown across him. Only his hands were moving, restlessly. His face turned to the lovely, radiant figure of the girl who entered. A tired voice said:

'Ah … it's you, Phil … come and let me look at you, darling. I didn't disturb your rest when I sent up for you, did I?'

Sally's heart beat violently. She closed the door behind her and walked over the soft carpet, dreading every second that drew her nearer that couch. When Martin saw her at close radius would be guess? Would he know?

For the first time she set eyes upon Martin Frome and a pang of sheer womanly pity shot through her. A tragedy indeed, if those long straight limbs were paralysed. He must have had a fine figure. His face and head were very attractive. A face thinned and whitened by recent suffering and confinement indoors, but the eyes were marvellously arresting, dark, brilliant, clever. Thick brown hair sprang crisply from a broad and intellectual forehead and he had the nicest mouth Sally had ever seen. Big, but generous and full of humour. Here was no cross, whining invalid, but a man who although he sees his life's work and happiness slipping from him, has retained a grip on life and on himself and can still smile. He was smiling now, drinking in every detail of Sally's appearance with pathetic pleasure.

'Glad I sent for you,' he said. 'Sweet, you're a sight for sore eyes.'

Sally swallowed hard.

'Am I?' she said, and laughed nervously.

'You certainly are. It's like bringing all the flowers with you. But rather a shame to take such a perfect flower out of the sunlight into this damned depressing atmosphere.'

There was a lump in Sally's throat. She began to wonder how that girl upstairs could withstand such a man as this ... could be tired of him when he said such things as that. Why, weren't they the sort of things she, Sally, had always wanted Rex to say and he had never quite known how? But then Rex wasn't an artistic lover. And Martin Frome was, a born one, which Sally was very quick to learn.

Impulsively she had laid a hand over one of Martin's.

'It isn't at all depressing to come and talk to you,' she said softly.

Then he stared.

'Why, Phil, you haven't said anything as nice as that to me for a long while.'

Sally felt terror-stricken.

'Haven't I?'

'No. You've been so chilly with me lately, darling.'

'I ... I'm so sorry.'

'Are you sure you aren't quite fed-up with me?'

'Sure. How are you this afternoon?'

'Just the same...' And now a quick, impatient sigh escaped Martin Frome. 'The eyes hurt a bit ... but they don't seem to hurt when I'm looking at you, my sweet. God, but I wish every time I hear that damn telephone that I could get on my feet and answer it and say: "Yes, I'm coming ... I'll be round at the hospital as soon as it's possible."'

He half regretted those words after he had spoken them. He was so well aware these days that Phil resented his work and his love of it. Hadn't he learned his bitter lesson? But Sally, full of a deep compassion and understanding ... swift to realise how exasperating it must be for this once busy surgeon to lie there and know that he was a useless log ... made a swift, warm reply:

'You poor dear ... it must be so ghastly...'

His thin face flushed. He looked up at her eagerly.

'You're very adorable to me this afternoon.'

And Sally flushed too ... with shame for the woman upstairs who could give less than this in the face of such urgent need.

'Phil, sweet, are you a little less angry with me, to-day, for smashing myself up and making things so rotten for you?' Martin was asking her.

And then there were tears in Sally's eyes, and she found herself whispering:

'How could I be angry at all?'

'But I thought you were ... oh, my darling, if you have a little of the old love left for me ... I think I could bear anything.'

His hands, still strong and sensitive and vital, were pulling her down to him now. His lips were against her hair, disarranging the big picture hat. And Sally fell on her knees beside the couch, bewildered, scared, torn with pity, and aghast by the lie that she was acting.

While she felt those fine, eager fingers caressing her hair and heard him murmuring the name 'Phil,' again and again, she knew very well that Philippa's scheme was not so impossible as it had seemed.

The first trial had been a tremendous success. *Too much of a success!*

She could feel his lips straying to her cheek and in panic she pushed him gently away, stood up, and nervously patted her hair into order and replaced the big hat with its drooping brim at the correct angle.

'I must go...' she said breathlessly.

He looked up at her. A faint, even cynical smile curved his mouth. That was typical of Phil. Any effort on his part to make love to her resulted in her immediately withdrawing into her shell and either laughing at him or imploring him not to disarrange her coiffure. Nothing Sally could have done could have more closely resembled her cousin's actions. Not that she had meant to be unkind. She would so willingly have stayed here and comforted him, and the fact that he had disarranged her hair mattered not at all. But those hungry searching lips frightened her. She stood there, her heart beating violently. He said:

'I hope I haven't done any damage.'

She felt her cheeks crimsoning.

'Oh, no, of course not.'

'Well, off you go and enjoy yourself. Who's to get the benefit of all the loveliness?'

She stammered:

'Lady Gordon-Bingham ... a garden party...'

Martin Frome's fine sensitive fingers played restlessly with the fringe of his rug. He gave a very tired smile.

'The Bingham woman's lucky ... to have you there ... tell her I said so.'

There was a choked little feeling in Sally's throat. Impulsively she thrust out a hand to him.

'I'll come and see you again. Have you something to read?... Oh, I suppose you mustn't use your eyes .. can I get you any-thing before I go...?'

She was stuttering, afraid of making blun-ders. And that was a little different from the cool, bored manner of Philippa, and made Philippa's husband look at Sally in some bewilderment. Something was wrong with his Phil and he didn't quite know what. Perhaps she was just trying to be kind. But she didn't love him any more. He knew that. That was a wound which she had given him and from which he would never recover. As usual, he jested in the teeth of pain.

'The only thing you can do for me is to go

on looking so beautiful, sweet. And if you can spare me an hour, come and tell me who fell in love with you at the party. Bye-bye.'

Sally turned and walked mutely out of the room.

She picked up her flowered chiffon skirt and almost ran up the wide staircase and back into Philippa's bedroom. Philippa had changed into a black and white suit and was sitting before her triple mirror trying the effect of a new black hat which had a rakish lace veil. She swung round as her cousin entered. The question she had meant to hurl at Sally died on her lips as she saw Sally's face. It was white and her eyes were enormous and full of tears.

Almost as soon as the door closed behind her Sally burst into tears.

'My dear Sally! What on earth's the matter?' asked Philippa, taking her arm and leading her to the bed.

Sally sat down weakly, swept off the big hat and hid her face in her hands.

'It's too terrible...'

'What is?'

'Poor Martin ... that poor dear...'

Philippa moved her head impatiently.

'Yes, yes, of course it's dreadful ... but you'll get used to it...'

'I couldn't. I could never get used to such tragedy ... and his courage ... that's what

41

hurts … the sight of his courage. And he loves you so … oh, Phil, how could you possibly want to leave him for a moment…?'

A very cynical retort rose to Philippa's lips, but she checked it. Sally was an emotional little idiot. Nothing irritated Philippa more than what she called 'slop'. But she had to control her irritation and be patient if she wanted Sally to open the gates of freedom for her.

She lit a cigarette, gave it to Sally, made her dry her eyes and smoke it and calm down.

'You mustn't take it so much to heart, my dear.'

Sally looked at her almost resentfully over her wet crumpled handkerchief which was pressed to her nose.

'Who wouldn't?'

'Quite so,' said Philippa smoothly. 'But as I say, you'll get used to it. Now, tell me how he received you. Did he think you were me?'

'Yes.'

Philippa's eyes shone with an almost unholy joy.

'Absolutely?'

'Yes.'

'But how *marvellous!* What did he say?'

Sally described the interview, then added:

'He wanted to kiss me … I felt so terribly sorry for him…'

'You mustn't be too sorry for him,' broke

42

in Philippa. 'Otherwise he'll smell a rat. I assure you I don't spend my whole time holding his hand. How could I?'

Sally stared at her cousin and wondered if there was any woman in the world so hard.

'Philippa, I just can't take this on – that's all!' at length she said.

Philippa's eyes narrowed and on her face was an expression which made her look at once very unlike Sally. She said:

'Oh, yes, you can, and you will.'

'I couldn't.'

'You must,' said Philippa, gripped Sally's shoulders and looked deeply into her eyes. 'You must … unless you want this home to crack up altogether.'

'Oh, what do you mean?'

'Just what I told you before you went downstairs. I can't go on … my nerves are in shreds. I'm at breaking point. You must be a little sorry for me as well as Martin. He *is* pathetic … frightfully brave and all that … but it just drives me crazy, having to sit there all day and be the bright consoler. Nobody in the world can help me but you. Please, please take it on just for a month, Sally. You'll be doing a good turn to us both. I'm sure Martin will get the benefit of your soft-heartedness.'

Dumbly Sally shook her head. But she was not allowed to speak. Philippa went on arguing passionately, as only Philippa knew how to argue when she wanted to get her own way. And finally she drew such a harrowing picture of her own unhappiness and the necessity that she should get away for a rest that Sally felt herself weakening.

'It can't do any harm to anybody,' Philippa finished. 'How can it? Nobody need know – even Denham.'

'But, Phil, if I … why can't I just stay as myself?'

'Because, my dear child, Martin wouldn't want his wife's cousin hanging round him. Added to which he'd be miserable at the thought that I'd gone away, and I'd be criticised and condemned by everybody. No, you must stay as "me". You'll have quite a marvellous time, I assure you, and I'll make it worth your while.'

Sally drew a deep sigh.

'Oh, I don't know.'

Philippa pleaded wildly all over again.

'It can't hurt you. Even if it's a sacrifice, do it for me. Your fiancé won't know. You can tell him you've got a job here as my secretary, and he can write to you here just the same.'

'And where will you go?'

Here, Philippa became cautious. She knew that there must be no mention of Ivor … of the real reason why she wanted frantically to get away. It must all be 'on the level' if she was to solicit help from Sally. She intimated that she would just 'slip away somewhere'. She might go to Killarney, to friends in Ireland who wouldn't give her away. Sally could write to her and keep her posted with all the news and she, Philippa, would just have a glorious month of rest and then at the end of it feel fit enough to return and go on with the strain of being married to Martin.

The longer that Sally listened, the more sorry she grew for Martin, rather than Philippa. Of course there were many arguments against her consenting to masquerade for a month as Mrs Martin Frome. On the other hand, there were things in favour of it. She had no job, barely enough to live on at the moment, and no prospects of marriage for a year ahead. In this house she would not only save money but earn it; apart from selfish motives, she could and *would* try and help Martin Frome through some of his difficult hours. She was also impressed by the assurance from Philippa that she would be virtually saving this home from catastrophe. It would be so terrible for Martin if Philippa let her nerves get the better of her and ran away altogether.

For a few moments Sally sat hesitating and brooding over the matter, allowing all Philippa's impassioned arguments to sink into her consciousness, and at the same time she thought of that man downstairs, waging his secret battle against pain and

45

boredom and the tragic knowledge that he had lost everything that had seemed to make life worth living.

It ended in Philippa winning the day. She had ended her pleading on a cunning note.

'I don't see why you should feel any compunction, my dear Sally ... it's a good deed even if it means acting a lie, and it's not going to hurt this Rex of yours at all. To begin with, he won't know, and to end with, he hasn't made things very easy for you, so why shouldn't you go your own way and make life easy for yourself? When this month's over, I'll see that you get a job as private secretary to one of my friends. You shall have a good time until you go back to South Africa to get married.'

Sally had to agree that it couldn't do anybody any harm and that there wasn't any real reason why she should account to Rex for everything that she did. Certainly he had not made any violent effort to get her back to South Africa. She did feel a little resentful about it.

'Are you very much in love with your future husband?' Philippa asked her.

Sally answered without hesitation:

'Of course.'

And then wondered as soon as she had said it whether it was strictly true. Was she so *very* much in love with Rex ... in the way that poets spoke of love and that she as a

46

very young girl had dreamed of love? As much, for instance, as Martin Frome appeared to be in love with his wife? With a passion, a hunger that sprang from the very depths of the heart and was not only a wild ache of the body.

She had thought that she felt like that about Rex when she first promised to marry him. And she had been miserable about leaving him in South Africa. But he was so practical and as a lover so unimaginative.

She had a fleeting vision of him in her mind's eye ... Rex, aged twenty-seven, not very tall, broadly built, with fair curly hair, a complexion which turned brick-red rather than brown in his native sunlight, and blue, rather short-sighted eyes. He wore horn-rimmed glasses for reading and writing.

He was quite good-looking, and very athletic. A favourite with other men; thoroughly at home in the smoking-room with his racy stories and hearty jokes. 'Hearty' ... yes, that's what one would call Rex. And, incidentally, when he wasn't in a good mood, he was inclined to sulk. Not altogether a heroic figure. Sally had known him to be very dogmatic and egotistical.

At the same time he could be a good friend, and, when he was keen, he put himself out to be charming. He had charmed Sally when they first met. She had been ready to melt at the first sign of tenderness from him. Somehow she had missed that tenderness lately. And that was why she had been afraid of a long-continued engagement, afraid that she might one day wake up and find that she didn't love Rex any more … afraid that she had grown apart from him.

She dismissed these thoughts almost immediately as disloyal and repeated her declaration that she was very much in love with her fiancé.

But she had known downstairs in the library, when she had knelt beside Martin Frome's couch and had heard him telling her how beautiful she was, that *that* was how she would have wished Rex to be. And *that* was what bored Philippa from Martin. How ironic! How topsy-turvy the whole world seemed.

Never had it seemed more so to Sally than this afternoon, when she sat in that golden room with Philippa and made the final arrangements to take her place as Mrs Martin Frome for a month.

3

Much later that evening, the big front door of the house in Harley Street closed upon the real Mrs Martin Frome. Very quietly Philippa Frome, with a suitcase and a cabin trunk, slipped away from all her liabilities, and without a single pang of compunction for the deception which she was practising upon her husband, joined her lover. Life offered a wild thrill of excitement at the moment and appeared to be prepared to allow her to 'both eat her cake and have it'.

Ivor Lexon was waiting for her at the Dorchester.

She had spoken to him on the telephone and only guardedly explained the situation. He scarcely knew what to make of it. The only thing of which he was aware was that his beautiful Philippa was no longer inaccessible and was coming to him. They were going away together for a whole month … on her money, of course … and there would be no scandal, no trouble, just a madly exciting, delirious four weeks in each other's company, with no one to say them nay.

From a window of Philippa's bedroom, Sally Browning, for the next month to be known as Philippa Frome, watched her cousin's taxi move away from the house, down Harley Street, and felt a moment of real terror. She almost opened the window and screamed to her cousin to stop.

This was crazy ... a mad thing to have undertaken ... she would never get away with it ... she'd be bound to make some mistake ... she couldn't go on deceiving Martin Frome, and when he found out there would be hideous trouble. She would be blamed, and rightly. It was a punishable offence. Martin might even send for the police ... these and a dozen other horrifying thoughts flitted through Sally's brain.

Then with shaking hands she lit a cigarette, smoked it and tried to steady her nerves. No use being foolish. She had done it now. She had given Philippa her word and she must carry on. Philippa was going to stay in town to-night but had promised to ring her up in the morning to know how things had gone off. She could, of course, wriggle out of it then, if she felt, after a night's sleep, that it was impossible to face a whole month of the masquerade.

'After to-morrow,' Philippa had said, 'you can write to me as Miss Maxwell. Yes, I shall use my maiden name. I can't go about the country as Mrs Frome. I'll keep you posted as to where I am, in case of emergency.'

'Of course it's all quite crazy,' Sally

reflected and began to laugh helplessly to herself as she sat down in front of the dressing-table and stared at her reflection.

How flushed and big-eyed she looked! And she felt exhausted with all the excitement and emotion. She would go to bed early. Philippa, before leaving, had put off a social engagement on her behalf. She would just see Martin for a while and then retire. And she must write a long letter to Rex, to-night. She didn't much like telling him lies, but she would have to explain why she were here in Harley Street, so she must say that she was acting as her cousin's private secretary.

There was nobody else except Rex with whom she need communicate. Now that her father was dead she was alone in the world. She could do what she wanted. That certainly made things easier in this case.

In her bag was a long list of things which she must memorise ... things which Philippa had told her ... careful instructions. Sally knew the names now of all Philippa's personal and intimate friends ... names of the members of the staff in the house ... of Martin's medical advisers ... of the various people whom she might have to meet and talk to. If she went warily, she would not give herself away. And on the desk was a calendar marking all Philippa's engagements which she must keep. She could, of course, always break them on the excuse that Martin needed her.

'You can be nice and attentive to Martin ... but don't be too sympathetic or he'll guess it isn't me,' had been one of Philippa's last statements.

Sally looked critically at her hair. She had not, of course, been near Lady Gordon-Bingham's garden-party. This afternoon she had been sitting at Antoine's in Dover Street, where Philippa's special hairdresser had made her hair look like Mrs Martin Frome's generally did ... parted on the left, and with two big crisp waves, and caught in a cluster of fashionable curls at the nape of the neck. Even the hairdresser had been deceived and had merely expressed some astonishment that 'madame's hair had got so badly out of place' since he last attended it.

There was Philippa's personal maid, Vera, to be dealt with yet. Fortunately this was Vera's day out, and so there had been nobody to pry when Philippa had packed to go away. And in the morning Vera would just bring in the tea and find Sally in her mistress's bed and take it for granted that it was ... her mistress. Nobody knew. *Not even Denham.* It had been decided between the cousins that it would not even be safe to let the trusted butler into the secret. They had hood-winked him nicely. For Philippa, in Sally's shabby suit and hat, had driven away as Miss Browning. And Sally, as Philippa, had told Denham that she had given her cousin some clothes, which accounted for the trunk. Sally had quaked a little when she had first addressed Denham, but the old butler had addressed her as 'madam' without hesitation. So now, if she played her part well, there was nothing further to worry about.

Gradually panic subsided and a feeling of interest in her new part crept over Sally. It was all rather exciting. And it really would be something worth doing if she could lighten some of the darkness of that poor dear downstairs.

She finished her cigarette, stubbed the ash in a tray on the dressing-table, and looked around her. A marvellous room, this, with its subdued colouring, pale peach satin curtains, peach-hued carpet, so rich and thick that one's bare feet sank into it, and walls and ceiling of delicate green. The wide divan bed had an arched headboard covered in brocade, with a cunning little shaded light affixed to it. There were soft green blankets and peach linen sheets, embroidered with the Frome crest, and a peach taffeta eiderdown. Queen Anne walnut furniture, pale, like polished gold, and a Queen Anne semi-circular dressing-table with a flounce of flowered taffeta in peach and green which toned with the rest of the room.

On the glass top stood a gleaming array of crystal bottles, jars, bowls, perfume, creams and lotions, all the dozen and one expensive trifles cherished by a woman of fashion. A wardrobe full of marvellous clothes. Philippa hadn't taken much away with her. And, leading out of the room, a bathroom on which a great deal of money had been spent and which had been designed specially to please Philippa, who liked something modern and out of the ordinary. Mirrored walls, a green sunken bath and a glass ceiling, floodlighted, through which one could see goldfish swimming. Sally thought it rather ridiculous and freakish, but Philippa had found it amusing.

No money had been spared to keep Cousin Philippa amused, decided Sally. On all sides were evidences of Martin's generosity and the will to please his *exigeante* young wife. And yet she gave way to nerves and deserted him when he was in most urgent need of her compassion and her love!

Somebody knocked on the door. A little nervously Sally said, 'Come in.'

A maid entered, in neat green uniform with cap and apron of coffee-coloured organdie. Sally, remembering Philippa's tuition, said:

'Oh, it's you, Harris.'

Harris was the parlourmaid who helped Philippa dress when her personal maid was out.

'What will you wear to-night, madam?' she asked.

'Oh, anything,' said Sally vaguely.

'You're dining in, aren't you, madam?'

'Yes. I want something quite simple.'

Harris sniffed as she went to the wardrobe. She didn't think any of madam's dresses particularly simple. They all cost a fortune. She didn't particularly like her mistress. None of the staff did. Philippa had a quick temper and a sharp tongue when she chose to use it. But she had moments of generosity, and Harris and Vera benefited by some of the 'cast-offs'. Harris's manner was as always, suave and deferential as she held out a black chiffon dress for Sally's inspection.

'This one, madam?'

'That will do.'

Then Sally added, keeping her face averted from the maid.

'What time is dinner?'

'When would you like it, madam?'

Sally looked at her watch … one of Philippa's watches … a costly little diamond wristlet. It said a quarter past seven.

'Oh, eight o'clock,' she said vaguely.

Harris put out a pair of black crêpe-de-Chine slippers with ankle straps, black chiffon stockings so fine that they were quite transparent, and black chiffon lingerie embroidered with jade. Everything was exquisite, and Sally almost gasped at the sight of so much extravagance, although she was

55

feminine enough to feel secret pleasure in it all. When it came to Harris wanting to know what jewellery she would wear she was momentarily baffled. That was something that Philippa had forgotten. She had not described the contents of her jewel case. But Sally passed it off by dismissing Harris and telling her that she would get something for herself.

Harris turned on the bath, threw in some scented crystals and then went downstairs to tell them in the servants' hall that 'my lady was in one of her moods'.

Sally found that the jewel case was locked and there was no key to fit it in any of the little drawers in the dressing-table. Possibly it was in Philippa's bag which she had taken away with her. That was annoying. She must mention that to Phil when she rang up in the morning.

Later, when she was bathed and dressed, Sally took a final look at her reflection in the long mirror. Was this Sally Browning ... that slim, lovely *soignée* creature with the perfectly waved head and the black dress that was a stroke of genius because of its sheer simplicity of line? Was this the shabby, ordinary Sally who had always longed for such clothes and occasionally envied women who could live this sort of life? It really was all very exciting!

This time last night she had been sitting in

a Bayswater boarding-house where she had taken a room on her arrival from South Africa. And later she had gone out to a cheap seat at a cinema with quite a nice girl in the same sort of circumstances as herself.

Sally thought of the boarding-house, of the atmosphere of genteel poverty, the smell of cabbage water and frying onions, the unattractive bedroom which had housed her while she disposed of the little house in Purley which had once been her home.

She had created a slight stir at Bayswater this afternoon, when, following upon Philippa's instructions, she had driven from Antoine's straight to the boarding-house, paid her bill, collected her writing case and one or two books and photographs which she wanted, then left the rest of her luggage in charge of Miss Potting, who ran the establishment, 'to be called for at a future date.'

And what a much greater stir she would have created if they had known why she had left so suddenly, if she could have told them the dramatic way in which she was changing places with her 'twin cousin'.

Came another knock at the door.

Sally turned with that slight feeling of nervousness which she still felt in this house. A man's voice said:

'The master would like to see you if you could come down, please, madam.'

That was Watson, Martin's valet.

'Tell him I'm coming now,' Sally answered.

And a moment later she was downstairs in the big library, where there was only one dim light burning. Martin Frome, lying as usual in the shadows, was propped up by pillows and wore a blue silk dressing-gown. He had been washed and changed for the night.

Beside the couch was a tray with some food which was barely touched.

Sally advanced to the couch and smile down at Martin.

'How are you to-night?'

'The same, thanks, my sweet. No need to ask how you are. You look beautiful. Do you get tired of me telling you how beautiful you are?'

That brought the colour to her cheeks, and she gave a little embarrassed laugh.

'I don't think any woman would get tired of it.'

That made him raise his brows. So often when he paid his wife a compliment she responded with sarcasm or an air of boredom.

Sally bent over the tray.

'Why, you've eaten nothing. You're going to have more than this, surely?'

He stared. It wasn't like Philippa to worry whether he ate or starved. She was generally too busy talking about herself ... when she came to see him.

'Darling!' he said with a faint laugh, 'if you

go on like this I shall begin to believe that you're quite concerned about me. That's twice in one day that you've...'

He stopped and checked himself. He decided that it was not very gallant of him to remind Phil of moments when she wasn't very nice to him at a time like this when she was. Of course he knew that she was a supreme egotist. He had known that for a long time and loved her in spite of it, with the hopeless love of a man who does not change his affections easily.

Sally blushed for Philippa. She was to blush a good many times for her cousin. Really, Philippa did not appear to behave with ordinary decency toward this man.

'Well, you are going to eat some more, aren't you?' Sally persisted.

'Do you want me to?'

'Of course.'

'Then I will.'

He managed to raise himself a little, and immediately Sally was there to put a cushion and a strong young arm behind his back.

He was astonished. She wasn't behaving like Philippa at all. Philippa would have rung for Watson if he wanted to be lifted. Lately she had shown quite plainly that she couldn't bear to touch him. What new spirit possessed that lovely body to make her more kindly, he wondered ... more like the woman that he had believed her to be when he had first fallen in love with her? Martin Frome did not seek far for the answer. He was only too happy to believe that something, somehow, had wrought a miracle in his Phil. He turned his head and kissed the satin smoothness of her arm.

'Thank you, angel.'

Sally drew away and sat down beside him. She lifted up the plate of cold chicken and handed it to him.

'Just a little more of this.'

He ate it, watching her, irritated because the light was bad and his eyes hurt. She was so fair, and so infinitely desirable, he wanted to drink in every detail of her face. Suddenly he said:

'Have you been in extra strong sunlight?'

'Why?'

'There are some freckles on the bridge of your nose that I've never seen there before.'

Sally gulped.

'It was very sunny … at the party this afternoon … and I took off my hat…'

'Ah! How was the party?'

'Oh, all right.'

'Was old Clifford Bingham there?'

Sally searched wildly in her mind for a suitable answer. Who was Clifford Bingham? Probably the husband or son … she didn't know which. And as she hadn't even been at the garden party she couldn't really tell Martin anything about it, so she murmured:

'M'm … Martin, eat some more chicken.'

'I've had a lot more.' He smiled and handed her back the plate. 'And I ate it specially to please you.'

'Would you like me to read to you or put on a record?'

He lay back on the pillows, his thin, tired face suffused with sudden colour.

'Don't be too nice to me, Phil.'

'I'm not... I'm no different...' she stammered and broke off helplessly.

'You are different,' he broke in, 'and I don't quite understand why. But don't give me hope when there isn't any. I'd grown almost used to the fact that you didn't really care about me any more.'

Sally sat silent. She could make no possible answer to that. She could see the naked pain in this man's eyes … mental, not physical pain. And she was desperately sorry for him. Then he said, in an altered voice:

'Sorry, sweet, I didn't mean to get all dramatic. Tell me some more about your party.'

The intensely sympathetic and generous streak which was in Sally made her alive and sensitive to his needs, the needs that were of the heart and soul so much more than of the body in this case. Here lay a man who was hopelessly in love with his own wife and afraid of annoying her by his devotion. That was a piteous thing. And Sally could

61

understand some of the miseries of Martin's repression, because was not she, herself, repressed? During her engagement to Rex she had so often longed for that closer, sweeter intimacy which can only take place between two people who thoroughly understand one another. And Rex had never been able to fill the void. Even when he held her in his arms in passionate moments and kissed her, there had been a romantic hunger in her which he could not appease.

Impulsively she said:

'You weren't being dramatic, Martin, and you mustn't say that I don't really care about you any more, because it isn't true.'

His eyes looked large and bright in his hollowed face. The thick dark hair clung damply to his forehead. He dragged his gaze from the beauty of the woman whom he believed to be his wife and looked through the open windows out at the blue summer dusk.

'Oh, I understand, Phil. It's bloody for you. I'm only a useless wreck.'

'Hush. You're going to get better.'

'Perhaps. Harold Stenning said this morning that he thought there was an improvement. He swears he'll have me walking in a few months.'

Philippa hadn't told her that. Sally felt genuine pleasure.

'Oh, but how wonderful, Martin.'

This tenderness of voice, this concern which he found so new and so disturbing, made Martin turn to her again and search her face. It seemed to him, like her voice, softer and sweeter. The only explanation he could put upon it was that she *did* care and that her recent hardness had been just a crust … a mask that she wore because she found it difficult to show her true feelings.

He said, huskily:

'Go and eat your own dinner, sweet. It's gloomy for you in here. Are you going out to-night?'

'No.'

'No theatre or party?'

'No.'

'But why not? Are you ill?'

She shook her head. She was terrified that she was going to weep.

'But you hate an evening without doing anything,' he persisted.

'I – I put off an appointment. I'd like to sit with you.'

'Oh, Phil!' he said.

There was so much pleasure in that simple exclamation that it defeated Sally's effort not to allow pity to get the better of her. Her eyes swam with tears, and Martin saw them. For a moment of white-hot blinding ecstasy he believed that his wife had still some real feeling left for him … something that would make him feel that it didn't matter that he

63

had been smashed up or that his beloved career had gone from him. Nothing could matter if Philippa loved him still.

He put out a hand and caught both of hers.

'Why, you're crying, Phil. I haven't seen you cry for years. Oh, my *sweet*.'

And then he pulled her down to him, and, before she could even try to prevent it, he was kissing away her tears with warm fervent kisses. He was saying:

'Love me a little … love me a little like you used to … if only you can!'

Sally did not draw away from him immediately. Frankly and unashamedly she was crying. Crying for pity of this man, for shame of Philippa and with no desire in her heart save to give him what comfort she could. For he had been stricken down at the prime of his manhood and at the height of his career, and it was as though he was a dead thing, save for his quick, fine brain and the passionate love of his wife which even her callous indifference and lack of response had not been able to destroy.

There was so much of the maternal in Sally. She loved little children. It seemed to her that this was a small boy, lying helplessly on his pillows, starved for affection. She put up a hand and stroked his hair.

'Hush,' she whispered. 'Don't distress yourself, my dear … of course.'

He lay quiet under the touch of her hand and shut his eyes. For an instant he was deluded into the belief that some miracle had been wrought in his lovely, heartless wife. She was not heartless. She was kind and human and she was crying ... for him!

He wanted to say so many things that he had repressed because he imagined they would annoy her. He wanted to hold her very close and kiss those lovely lips which had grown suddenly kind for him. There was so much pent up in him waiting to be released, to find expression. But after all those months, after so many rebuffs, so many bitter moments in which Philippa had destroyed his passion by showing that she was bored ... what more destructive to a man's love than that? ... he could not easily break through his own reserve.

He had grown cynical because she had made him so. Much as he adored ... adoration was tempered now by that faint contempt of her character which her own actions had bred in him. She had done so many little things to hurt him and shake his belief in her. It was only natural if he had grown suspicious of her more kindly moments. For had it not been proved to him in the past that Phil was particularly kind only when she wanted something?

To-night she was unusually sweet and concerned, but he told himself not to be a fool, not to work himself up into a fever-heat over it. She would end by ridiculing his passion … and, of course, by hinting at some new whim which she wanted to satisfy.

Of his own accord he suddenly pushed her gently but firmly away from him. He must get a grip on himself and not let her tears or her unwonted softness stir him too greatly. He did not wish to be hurt all over again.

'Lord save us, this won't do, Phil,' he said in a changed voice. 'No wonder you get fed up with sitting by my bedside. Sorry, sweet, I don't usually go in for moaning. But why the tears? What does the spoiled baby want now?'

That question, on a forced note of gaiety, would have satisfied the real Philippa. She would have risen to her feet with a sigh of relief and then expressed her wishes. But in some strange way it hurt Sally to the depths of her being. It hurt her because she knew that if Martin spoke like that it must be because he imagined it was expected of him. It was what Philippa expected. And, because of Philippa, Sally's very womanhood was outraged.

Her tears had been sincere, and he took it for granted that she 'wanted something'. Well, she was in Philippa Frome's shoes, and as Philippa she must behave. But not too much like Philippa, because it was so foreign, so distasteful to her. She wanted nothing and she said so.

'The spoiled baby has everything that she needs, thank you,' was her reply, in as light a tone as she could muster. She stood up and turned away, dabbing fiercely at her eyes with her handkerchief.

Martin's brooding gaze followed her. He might almost have imagined that she was piqued because he had mastered his emotions. But he knew her too well for that. She disliked emotion. And above all she hated being made love to. That caressing way in which she had stroked his hair just now ... that lilt in her voice, begging him not to distress himself... God! that was not at all like his Phil! There was something at the back of it. And he didn't quite know what. But he did know that he refused to be drawn up to a pinnacle of hope only to be flung down with the bitterness of disillusion again.

He continued to talk to her in that half-tender, half-bantering way in which he usually addressed his wife these days.

'You're not your usual bright self, darling. Who upset you at the party? Did somebody have a better dress than yours?'

Sally bit her lip. Now he was being hateful. No. This was not the real Martin. This was the Martin that Philippa had made of him. She had enough sensibility to realise that. She tried to be as Philippa would be, shrugged her shoulders, turned back to him and said:

'No, I'm just off colour.'

'But you look so marvellous. I don't think I've ever seen you so brown and fit.'

'Oh, I'm all right, but...'

'Well?'

He smiled up at her. A very tired smile. He was waiting for the request which he was confident would eventually be made. Possibly her allowance was overdrawn this quarter, or she wanted to change her car. Well, she *was* a spoiled baby, and he knew it. But he gave her what she wanted. Fortunately he had plenty of money ... money of his own and which his father, an eminent surgeon before him, had left Martin, as well as the handsome income which he had been making these last few years as a consultant.

Even if he could never work again, he could still afford to give Philippa the luxuries which were the breath of life to her. That was about all that was left to him ... the pleasure of being able to give. Before his accident there had been only two things in his life that counted. His wife and his work. Now only the former was left to him.

4

It was only since his accident that Martin Frome had really begun to realise to the fullest extent how little his wife really cared for him. Perhaps that was because he had more time to lie here and think about it and he was in greater need of her love. But while he had been working hard the true aspect of their marriage had not been quite in focus. It had been a little blurred in the rush of work. Now he saw it very much in its true perspective.

He was too proud a man to complain or to spoil any of her pleasures. He let her go her own way. Although there were moments when he disliked the thought of her friendship with men like Ivor Lexon. But he did not allow himself to be suspicious of her fidelity. He had not a jealous temperament, and these days he took it for granted that a helpless, bedridden wreck of a man must not expect a woman like Philippa to give him all her pity and attention. She was lovely and gay and adored pleasure. Other men must be allowed to take her out. That was only natural.

The thing for him to do was to make a

mighty effort to get well again. Yes, he must get on his feet and walk and do away with all this gloom and then his Phil would be a little more amused by him. Poor child, how could he expect her to sadden her life because his had changed so sadly? Thank God, Stenning, who was one of the biggest authorities in the world on paralysis, had given him a word of hope this morning. And Dacre Cheniston, the well-known ophthalmic surgeon, fully expected his eyes to recover.

Cheniston was one of Martin's great friends. It was such a pity that Phil didn't like him. Perhaps that was because Cheniston's wife wasn't quite her sort. Personally Martin had a great regard for Jan Cheniston. She was a quiet, shy little thing, with none of Philippa's brilliance. But she was a wonderful wife to Dacre, and it was with her help that he had built up a second great career for himself after the first had been shattered by a scandal in the past.

Women could be so marvellously loyal and helpful.

It was only natural that Martin should turn his thoughts now and again to the Chenistons and take it for granted that, if anything like this had happened to Dacre, Jan would never have left his side. But it was rarely that he indulged in thoughts like these.

'Well, darling, is there anything wrong?' he said after a long pause during which Sally

70

had been standing there, no longer weeping but frowning a little as though perplexed.

'I'm all right,' she repeated.

And she told herself that in future she must not let compassion get the better of her. She would be kind, but not too kind. She must remember that Philippa had said:

'You mustn't be too sorry for him ... otherwise he'll smell a rat...'

So she conquered her desire to be very gentle and assumed a light manner, to match Martin's own.

'I think I'm a bit tired, Martin. That's all. I must be ... I'm not usually tearful, am I?'

'Far from it.'

The butler entered the room.

'Dinner is served, madam.'

'Run along and eat a good meal, darling,' said Martin.

'I'll be back,' said Sally.

'Well, don't if there's anything more amusing...' he began.

'No,' she interrupted. 'I'll spend an hour with you.'

And she supposed that *that* was being too attentive. But she couldn't do less. Impossible, with the thought of his helplessness and pain ever before her and a memory which she could not banish of the ecstasy on his thin face when she told him she would like to sit with him. She wondered if she could ever forget the tone of his voice as he had begged her to love him 'just a little'.

She did not enjoy that lonely dinner in the big dining-room. It was perfect food, perfectly served by well-trained servants. But she had no appetite. She was nervous, half-conscious all the while of the butler's scrutiny and ever wondering who would be the first person to detect the fact that she was not Mrs Martin Frome.

She almost wished herself back in the boarding-house in Bayswater. Pleasant though it was to exchange badly cooked joint and rice pudding for iced melon, fish soufflé, creamed veal and an ice, she had at least suffered the poorer food with nothing on her conscience. And now there was so much on it – Rex in particular. What on earth Rex would say to this masquerade she dared not think.

She was not sure that she wanted to think too much about Rex at the moment. The thought of him did not bring her much happiness to-night. He had failed her. Yes, she could not help but admit that. Failed her when she had most wanted him, now that she was alone in the world. And even before her father's death in the first flush of their engagement, he had failed her, not once, but many times as a lover. She could not, for instance, imagine herself kneeling beside Rex's bed, crying, and Rex kissing away her tears. He would have just squeezed her hand and patted her shoulder and said:

'Why the waterworks? Don't cry, old girl. Give us a kiss.'

Jovial, ever practical Rex. What had made her fall in love with him? Perhaps the fact that there had been nobody else. She had met so few eligible men in her constricted existence, tied to domestic duties and her old father. She had longed for romance, for a lover, and Rex had seemed to come at the psychological moment and fill the bill.

Here Sally stopped thinking. This was flagrant disloyalty and tantamount to a confession that she no longer loved Rex. She must school her thoughts quickly. She was just being foolish, allowing herself to be influenced by Martin Frome's glamorous personality and the atmosphere in this house.

With some trepidation, Sally returned to the library and to Martin.

'Shall we have some music?' she suggested.

'I'd love it,' he said.

Sally walked to the big radio-gramophone. She recalled what Philippa had told her about Martin's tastes. He had played the piano in his youth and was a lover of the classics, particularly of Wagner.

'Would you like one of your Wagner records?' Sally asked, feeling rather like a well-tutored child remembering its lesson.

'I'd love it, darling,' he said.

His gaze was no longer fixed on the slim

figure in the black evening dress. He lay against his cushions gazing dreamily at a big portrait in oils which hung on the wall opposite his couch. It hung in shadow but he knew every line of the exquisite face and form which had been reproduced in soft, lovely colours by one of the leading painters of the twentieth century. It was Philippa's mother with Philippa in her arms, aged two or three. Philippa's father had given it to her before he died. She would have put it in an attic because she disliked portraits and had no particular affection for her mother, whose quick temper and wayward nature had clashed with her own in later years.

Martin, however, had rescued the portrait and hung it here because he loved it. It was not that he had been particularly devoted to his mother-in-law, or deplored her loss very greatly when she died a year ago. But the picture of the mother and child was, in itself, a beautiful thing. The painter had captured a certain moving spirit of tenderness which appealed to him. And there was a strong resemblance between Philippa and her mother.

Martin liked to look at the beautiful woman holding the curly-headed child against her breast and to imagine that it was Philippa with his child in her arms. He had wanted a child more than anything on earth. The vision remained. He never lost

74

the love of this portrait or the motherhood that it stood for. But he had long since trampled on his desire for a child because Philippa had raised so many objections, had shown such a terror of child-bearing and such loathing for the thought of all that it entailed, that he had never insisted.

Sally opened the lid of the big electric machine and for a few moments stared down at it baffled. Here was one of the things that it would not have entered Philippa's head to tell her. Sally had not the slightest idea how to put on that gramophone. She stood there, puzzling, her cheeks growing hot with confusion. After a pause came Martin's voice:

'What's wrong?'

She stammered:

'I ... I don't know ... what's happened to the switch, do you think?'

'It was all right this evening. Watson got the time and news for me at six o'clock.'

For a moment Sally's heart played funny tricks with her. It would be too ludicrous if over a small thing like this the whole of hers and Philippa's schemes went awry.

To her enormous relief Watson entered the room at this moment with a liqueur brandy for his master. Then Martin said:

'Take a look at the wireless, Watson. Mrs Frome thinks it's gone out of order.'

Watson advanced to the radio. He was a small, thin little man with an expressionless face. If there was one person in the world he cared for, it was Martin. He would have laid down his life gladly for 'the doctor', to whom he was as much nurse-attendant as valet these days. And if there was one person he despised it was the doctor's wife. As he so often described her to the folks at home: 'Pretty as paint and ugly-natured as the devil, and the doctor is too ruddy good for her.'

He at once switched on the radio-gramophone.

'It's quite all right,' he said, eyeing Sally a trifle sourly.

She gave him the only smile he had ever had from 'Mrs Frome'. Philippa detested Watson, possibly because she knew that he despised her.

'Thank you so much, Watson,' Sally said, in the charming way in which she always addressed servants. 'How silly of me … it seems quite all right, doesn't it?'

He stared and then turned away, telling himself that the doctor must have given my lady an extra cheque to make her so full of honey.

Sally, left alone with Martin, looking through the records, said:

'Nice little man, isn't he?'

'Good God!' said Martin. 'I thought you loathed him.'

Sally blushed. She wondered how many times her face would scorch with colour in this house. Another trifling mistake, but how on earth could she know exactly what to say and what not to say? It was really too confusing. She covered her mistake by saying:

'I think I've liked him better lately.'

'That's good. I've always told you he was a decent little blighter and very attached to me.'

Sally put on a record.

She, herself, adored music and particularly Wagner. They had had a gramophone at home and Sally had often saved religiously to buy the expensive records which were generally outside her means. She chose the Overture to the *Meistersingers*.

'Would you like that, Martin?' she asked.

'Fine!' he said.

She sat down in a chair by the couch and they listened in silence to the splendid sonorous music. Sally was particularly moved tonight by the wistful beauty of the Prize Song which had always been one of her favourite melodies. It seemed full of almost unbearable longing. She knew how it must appeal to Martin Frome in his present state. She found it difficult not to talk to him about it, rhapsodise when it was over. But she had to remember that Philippa had warned her that she knew nothing whatsoever about classical music and only liked dance records.

She was quite resentful when Martin said:

'It must be boring you so horribly, darling.

Don't play any more Wagner. Put on a fox-trot.'

She had to check herself. She wanted to tell him that that would be desecration ... that she could sit here half the night listening to the music that he loved and that she shared his understanding and his appreciation. And there was Rex in South Africa, who, like Philippa, only understood and appreciated jazz! Life seemed full of these small ironies.

Sally grew conscious of something approaching irritation. Yes, it was really maddening this not being able to be herself ... and having to act the part of a character totally different from her own. Strange how different she and Philippa were, although physically so alike. And it was with some regret that she reflected that the real Sally could have been very great friends with Martin Frome.

Martin smiled at her.

'No dance music?'

'Not to-night.'

'Still not feeling very well?'

'Oh, I'm fine now, thanks. I think I'll go to bed.'

'Darling, you must be ill... I usually have to scold you for keeping such late hours.'

'I was very late last night,' she muttered, and felt that she would scream if she had to prevaricate any further.

'Oh, well, it'll do you good. Run along,' he said.

She felt more annoyed than ever. She did not want to leave him alone. She knew how very protracted and tedious the hours must seem to him. And she wanted to go on playing classic music and to discuss it all with him. She dared not do any of these things.

Really, she half made up her mind to tell Phil when she rang up in the morning that she must come back. Not for anybody's sake could she go on with this deception. It was too nerve-racking, for one thing, and too difficult for another. She had not the slightest desire to behave like the real Philippa and every desire to be herself.

Mental anxiety had made Sally curt and unresponsive with Martin since dinner, and quite different from the compassionate Sally who had wept in his arms a few hours ago. But that did not seem strange to Martin because he had not entertained much hope of her thawing ... for more than a few minutes.

'Doing something exciting to-morrow?' he asked.

She stood beside him, and for an instant met his gaze fully. The shaded lamp showed how tightly the skin was drawn over his cheek-bones, and how thin he was. He was a man sick to the soul ... and yet that big humorous mouth of his could grin at her

79

cheerfully like a schoolboy. Speechless pity for him enveloped her again. She tried to answer his question idly.

'Oh, I don't know … a lot of things.'

'Spare a minute or two for me when you can, sweet. Stenning is starting new treatment for me and old Dacre is coming in the morning. With any luck I may be allowed a bit more light and be allowed to read shortly.'

'I'm glad,' said Sally.

Then she looked away from him and found herself staring at the oil painting that faced the couch. With a sense of shock she gazed more closely at it. Was that Phil? Phil with a *child* … but she didn't think … no … of course not .. how foolish of her … that was Philippa's mother.

'Aunt Jenny,' thought Sally. 'Aunt Jenny with Phil… Good Lord!... I remember her when I was about that age, three or four … when we first played together in the nursery.'

It seemed uncanny to be standing here looking at her aunt's portrait … poor old Daddy's sister whom he had described as being 'a selfish egotist' … like Philippa.

Sally had to bite her lips to prevent herself from saying to Martin:

'That's my aunt … father's youngest sister … aren't we all absurdly alike, she and Phil and I…'

Instead of which she said:

'Good night, Martin. I hope you sleep

well, my dear.'

He held out a hand.

'You've been very sweet to me.'

Her fingers curved within his.

'I've done nothing.'

He looked at her searchingly as though something about Phil to-night was worrying him, baffling him. Something indefinable which disturbed his consciousness. Something unfamiliar ... or was it that occasionally, unexpectedly, she became the incarnation of a sweet and hopeless dream that was almost as familiar as the realities in his life?

He pulled her a little down to him. She bent at once and kissed him on the forehead. She could not bring herself to bestow a more intimate caress. Not because she disliked the thought. There was nothing repugnant about Martin. On the contrary there was so much that attracted her. But he was a complete stranger and her position was an extremely embarrassing one.

If he had expected a warmer embrace he did not say so. He let go her hand and she walked quickly from the room and closed the door behind her.

Martin's gaze, restless, tormented, returned to the portrait of the mother and child before him. Then almost savagely he rang the bell for Watson to come and take him to his room.

5

In spite of her working conscience, Sally slept dreamlessly in the softest and most luxurious bed on which she had ever lain. Different from all the other beds ... the old-fashioned austere little one with mahogany rails which had been hers from a child at home ... the uncomfortable camp bed which had been put up for her in the Trenchmans' bungalow in South Africa when she had visited Rex, and that awful one at the boarding-house with the fumed oak head board and knobbly mattress!

As soon as she woke, Sally stretched her arms above her head with a little sigh of pure luxurious contentment, nestled against the big square down pillows, and fingered the fine peach linen sheets with their embroidered hems, and the thick fleecy blankets. Lovely things! Lovely rooms – full of soft peachy light, sunshine filtering through delicate net and taffeta curtains.

The next thing that happened was that Sally caught sight of her finger nails and gave a little murmur of distaste. That blood red varnish ... hateful!... Philippa's own pet lacquer. And she had been warned that she must allow her nails to grow longer because Philippa had Chinese points which Sally thought atrocious. Her own were short and as a rule she used a natural pink polish.

Then the door opened and a maid came in and set a tray on a table beside the bed. A neat girl with a pale face and dark, braided hair. She wore no cap but only a tiny organdie apron over a pale green dress. Sally sat up and became alert. This must be Vera, Philippa's personal maid. It would be a test if Vera detected nothing amiss when she looked at her mistress.

Vera barely looked twice, however. She just said: 'Good morning, madam,' and busied herself folding up clothes. Personally she was a little astonished because madam's stockings were hanging neatly over a chair and there was not so much tidying to do as usual.

Sally returned the greeting and poured herself out some tea, admiring the charming china, apple-green, eggshell thin, the embroidered cloth on the tray. There was a slice of lemon in the saucer but no milk. That was a little difficult. Philippa apparently liked lemon in her tea, Russian fashion. Sally loved lots of milk. She wondered how on earth to get over the difficulty without giving herself away, but decided to do nothing for the moment, and sipped the China tea with a slight grimace.

She said:

'Would you draw the curtains, please?'

Vera turned and raised her brows.

'I'm sorry, madam,' she said huffily. 'But you particularly asked me yesterday not to draw them because the sun hurt your eyes.'

Another of Sally's blushes. She lay back on the pillow and groaned to herself. Dear, oh dear, what a difficult person cousin Phil must be and how complex an example to emulate! But she could not put up with this peachy dusk, when the sun was shining so brilliantly this summer morning. Sally, with her worship of the 'out-of-doors', was firm about that.

'Well, I think this morning we'll have them drawn, Vera. It's so lovely.'

The maid drew back the curtains and flooded the big beautiful room with golden light. There was no accounting for madam's whims, she thought. She was as variable and as changeable as the English weather.

'What will you wear this morning, please, madam?'

That perplexed Sally for a moment. She really had not had time to discover all the secrets of Philippa's wardrobe. She had to be cunning in her new rôle. She murmured:

'Oh, anything.'

Vera possessed her soul in patience. She threw a somewhat resentful glance at the slim fair-haired girl in the bed. It struck her suddenly that madam was putting on some of that sunburn colouring you could buy in bottles, and putting it thick! She hadn't noticed before how very brown she was. Too brown! It didn't look natural in Vera's estimation.

'You'll be going out, I suppose, madam?'

Sally searched her brain and managed to remember that Philippa's engagements for to-day were many and that the first one was 'a fitting' in Bond Street for hats.

'Yes. I've got a fitting at eleven.'

Vera produced a smart grey flannel walking suit.

'How about this and the grey and red spot silk blouse, madam?'

'That'll do.'

'What time will you get up, madam?'

'Now,' said Sally.

Then Vera wondered if the world had come to an end. Madam was born lazy. She liked to lie here reading her papers and new society journals and telephoning her friends (and lovers, so they said in the servants' hall) and she had never, *never* been known to get up for breakfast!

Sally, always on edge in this house, was quick to see the expression on the maid's face. Oh lord! She had done wrong again. Presumably Phil breakfasted in bed. But Sally could not lie here doing nothing. She was by nature energetic and liked exercise. She wanted to be up and out. She was all the more determined, as soon as Philippa telephoned, to decline carrying on with this farce.

She averted her gaze from the maid.

'I shall get up to breakfast this morning, Vera,' she announced. 'I've got a lot to do to-day.'

'Just the usual grape fruit and thin toast, madam?'

Sally, who had a healthy appetite, flung her eyes heavenwards.

'Yes,' she said.

And wondered if the first thing she did would not be to go round to Lyons and have a large dish of eggs and bacon. Philippa was banting, was she? Surely she had no need to, with her slim figure! What an insight this was into the futile, artificial life led by women like Philippa Frome. Then Sally remembered Martin. Her face softened.

'How is Mr Frome this morning, Vera! Will you please find out for me?'

Vera went out of the room. She had attended Mrs Frome for two years and thought she knew her fairly well. But she decided now that she would never know her. One moment she was cursing and swearing and making herself an objectionable cat, and the next she was as sweet as honey, asking after the doctor's health! It was the first time she had ever asked Vera after him, and the poor gentleman so handsome, too. Vera had a secret passion for the doctor. Everybody on the staff had shed a tear when the doctor had been brought back from the home after his accident. But Vera had never seen Mrs Frome shed a tear. She would be too afraid of her eyelash black running! Oh, she was as pretty as paint and had clothes that made Vera lick her lips and that's why she stayed on, otherwise she'd never stand the whims of such a pussy!

She spoke to Watson, Martin's valet, whom she met on the stairs. Watson listened to what she had to say and sniffed.

'Tines have changed. It never struck me that her ladyship cared whether the doctor lived or died. And so sweet she was to me last night when she told me that the radio wouldn't work. Must be afraid that all her bad temper's putting lines on her face. Oh well! Tell her that he's passed a good night and is showing signs of improvement. Perhaps that'll upset the sweetness. I bet she's keen for him to go to his grave so that she can marry that black-haired chap who's forever in the house!'

Vera made a suitable reply and returned to her mistress's bedroom. She delivered Watson's message to Sally. Sally, glancing through a new *Tatler* which had been brought to her, exclaimed:

'Good news!'

Then Vera, a trifle guiltily, wondered

whether Mrs Frome was human after all and retired to prepare madam's breakfast, and tell the rest of the staff that her ladyship, as Philippa was known to them, was for some inexplicable reason like treacle this morning.

Sally, unaware that she had been anything other than ordinarily civil and correct, waited for the next couple of hours in a fever of impatience for the telephone call which did not come. She had to ring up the modiste and put off her fitting because she was loth to leave the house until the call came through. Surely Philippa *would* ring! She had promised to. She must come back and take up her position in this house. Even if she had to practise rigid self-control and do without her holiday, she must come back. Sally had decided that. It was impossible to go on like this.

Last night, before she went to sleep, she had tried to write to Rex and found it very hard to be honest, to be herself, and not let him know what she was really doing for her cousin. Besides, Martin and his whole personality disturbed her too vastly.

She had also found it difficult to pen the usual words of passion and longing to her lover in South Africa. It was like penning them to somebody who would not understand ... could not understand that kind of love ... whereas Martin Frome ... but oh!

she must not think in that way about Martin. He was Philippa's husband and just a person to whom she must be kind until Philippa came back. Then she would go away from this lovely house in which she did not really belong, and return to her own life.

Midday came and still Philippa had not telephoned. Sally's heart was sinking. Why didn't she ring? Where was she? What had she in her mind?

Sally thought it her duty to go and see Martin apart from any personal pleasure that she would get out of the visit. So soon after noon she went down to the library and found Martin there in a dressing-gown on his couch. He was waiting for his friend, Dr Stenning, to come and pay his morning call.

The library was a little lighter than usual. It was quite a shock to Sally to see how light it was compared with yesterday. Martin's fine features, sharpened by suffering, were clearly discernible, and she could see the expression of pleasure that crossed his face when she entered the room. That sort of look which could not fail to bring a little ache of compassion to Sally's throat.

'Good morning, my dear,' she said. 'I was so pleased to hear from Watson that you had a better night and that there is an improvement.'

His eyes shone. He had thought that perhaps yesterday's good humour had been a passing phase with her and that her sweetness meant nothing ... nothing more than a wish for some new toy. He had not deluded himself. Yet here she was, more charming than ever this morning. He felt suddenly happier, stronger than he had been since his accident. He held out a hand to her.

'I can't tell you how much better I'm feeling this morning, sweet,' he said eagerly. 'And my eyes ... I can bear the light to-day without pain. And I can see you quite plainly. So the optic nerves are not in such bad condition after all. Isn't that splendid?'

'Marvellous, but oughtn't you to be wearing a shade ... or glasses?' Sally asked and came to the side of the couch and placed her slender fingers in his outstretched hand. He clung to them warmly.

'I daresay I may have to if I go out in the sun. But not indoors.'

'When will you be allowed out?'

'Quite soon, I hope. I'm going to ask Stenning to let me go for a drive with you. That is ... if you can spare me half an hour.'

Sally, who never failed to be shocked by such proof of Philippa's callousness, answered without hesitation.

'Spare you half an hour! But I should think so. And much longer.'

A warm glow went through the thin, wasted body of the man. He bent his head and kissed her hand.

'Phil, it's like old days to hear you talk like that.'

The touch of his lips against her hand and the tone of his voice brought the hot colour to her cheeks and throat. Poor dear Martin! How starved he was ... how starved for affection!

Perhaps she was being dangerously nice to him and everything would be discovered ... but she could not force herself to treat him with the indifference which Philippa had shown.

'You must tell Dr Stenning to let you out as soon as possible. The sun would do you so much good, Martin.'

'Not so much good as the sight of you.'

His brilliant eyes travelled over her with an intentness which embarrassed her. Was he detecting some difference between her and the real Philippa? But no. He merely said:

'You look grand in that grey suit and this...' He touched the red spotted bow of her blouse... 'How sweet it is against your sunburn. By Jove, Phil, I don't think I've ever seen you look so fit. Who'd think you had so many late nights and gay parties? You look like a girl ... a child who eats bread and milk and fruit and goes to bed every night at sundown.'

Sally laughed.

'What a quaint thought. Well, perhaps if it does me so much good I'd better give up the parties and take to the bread and milk and early bed!'

He had not known her so kind, so gay with him, or so purely friendly since the earliest days of their engagement. His Phil had started to be spoiled and unreasonable so soon after their marriage. What had wrought the change? What miracle had transformed her into the girl with whom he had fallen so desperately in love ... before he got to know her well ... oh yes! he had to admit that he had not been able to love Philippa so blindly *after* their marriage. Her own behaviour had soon tinged his love with bitterness. This was such a sudden change, because only yesterday ... or was it the day before ... she had rushed in here to bid him a cool and careless good morning, asked permission to buy something that she wanted and rushed out again, leaving him to feel that it would have been better had the car smashed him up altogether and left her free.

He wondered what was happening to that Lexon fellow who was always about the place. He could never understand why Philippa liked Ivor Lexon. He was such a typical gigolo ... just a good-looking cad who sponged on pretty women who had nothing better to do than dine and dance with him.

'Lexon been here lately?' he asked.

And he asked it, not because he wanted to, or even wanted the thought of Lexon to spoil his pleasure in Philippa's present attitude, but because he thought that it would please her. He told himself that the last thing he must do was to take advantage of her friendliness and drive her away. He would have to go so warily. One false step and he might irritate her. He must not let that radiant beauty, that beauty and allure appeal to him too strongly. He must remember that she hated being made love to and it would annoy her if allowed himself to be a sentimental fool. So, deliberately, he asked after Lexon.

Sally hesitated, looking away from Martin, and then answered:

'Yes.'

'Didn't you tell me he was taking you to Ranelagh to-morrow?'

'I … oh, I've put it off.'

'Put off your adored polo? But why?' he asked incredulously.

'Oh, I don't know,' faltered Sally. 'I just don't want to go to-morrow.'

She then changed the conversation and admired the flowers on the table beside the fireplace. Martin lit a cigarette and pondered a moment. Perhaps Phil and Lexon had quarrelled. She seemed rather loth to discuss him. All the better if she didn't see so much of him. Not that he didn't trust her but he couldn't stand that fellow!

Sally, bending to inhale the fragrance of

the pink roses in the blue Chinese bowl, was thinking:

'Why, why doesn't Phil telephone? Surely she can't mean *not* to! And she's got the key of the jewel case too. Oh, how I hate all this intrigue and deception.'

'Aren't you going out, darling?' came Martin's voice.

'I'd like to wait until Dr Stenning's been and see what he says about you.'

'That's altogether charming of you, my sweet. By the way, if I'm going to be allowed out soon, we shall want the Daimler. I asked you the other day to tell Smith to have it decarbonised. You did, didn't you?'

'M'm!' said Sally, and made a mental note of the fact that she must see about it in case Philippa had forgotten. Smith was Martin's chauffeur. Sally knew that. She had a list of the servant's names.

She came back to Martin's bedside. Sudden curiosity made her question him.

'I wonder when you'll be able to walk again, Martin.'

Delighted in her show of interest in him, he answered cheerfully:

'Oh, with all this massage and treatment I may get on my feet in a few weeks from now. Stenning thinks so and from my own diagnosis of the case, I see no reason why I shouldn't be walking with a couple of sticks in a month from now.'

'That's fine.'

'Grand if it's going to matter to *you*.' Then he made haste to add: 'But of course it will. It's no fun for anything as lovely and young as you to have a wreck for a husband. That damnable accident … what a tragedy it was…'

'But not your fault, Martin.'

He gave her a quick puzzled look.

So often since his accident Philippa had hinted that he *was* to blame, said that he must have driven carelessly. But it had been Smith's half day and there had been that urgent case at Richmond. They had phoned to tell him that the patient had had a serious relapse. True, he had gone a little fast considering the night was foggy. But he had wanted to save that life. In doing so he had so nearly lost his own! His first thought on recovering consciousness in hospital had been for his patient … his first words, a request that another surgeon consultant should go down to Richmond at once. His second thought had been one of supreme thankfulness that his wife had not been in the car with him. It would have been so awful if he had hurt *her*.

'Have you changed your mind, then, about the accident, Phil? You rather drove it home that I *was* to blame.'

Sally, without knowledge of all the details of that unhappy smash, answered carefully:

'What does it matter now whose fault it was? The main thing is that you're going to get better.'

'Darling, when you're as nice to me as this you make me feel inclined to pray to the Almighty to effect an immediate and miraculous cure so that I can jump to my feet this moment and embrace you.'

He spoke lightly but she could see the flame in his eyes. She was beginning to conquer her desire to weep for sheer pity. She just smiled and said:

'Let us all pray, my dear!'

He controlled the longing to carry her hand to his lips again.

'Run along out into the sunshine, angel,' he said huskily. 'Don't waste your time in here the whole morning. I'll let you know what Stenning says.'

It struck her suddenly that she would rather not meet Dr Stenning. She was supposed to know him. It would all be very embarrassing. On the other hand she just could not leave the house in case Philippa's call came through. She was in a quandary.

Then, to her infinite relief, the butler entered the library and told her 'that a lady wished to speak to her on the phone.'

'Will you excuse me, Martin,' said Sally, and hurried from the room.

Martin Frome drew a deep breath after she had gone and lay still, smoking and thinking, brooding over the incomprehensible ways of woman and particularly of his wife. Something had put her in an adorable humour, and he could but praise heaven for it. It was quite certain that he loved this wayward and unreliable wife more than anything on God's earth, and if she was feeling a little remorseful for her recent conduct and anxious to be nice and to make up for it, it was the surest way of helping him to recover and to recover with all possible speed.

Up in the boudoir Sally lifted up the white painted receiver and said:

'Hullo, who is it?'

'*Me*, but don't say a word,' came the reply.

Sally thanked God devoutly. So it *was* Philippa.

'I've been waiting for this all the morning.'

'I couldn't ring before. I've been too hectic.'

'You've got to come back at once.'

'For God's sake, shut up you little fool. Anybody can hear.'

'No. My door's shut.'

'Well, some of those precious maids aren't above putting their ears to the keyhole.'

'I'll be careful. I presume this *is* a private line?'

'Yes, you can be certain I have my own line,' came Philippa's voice with a slightly vicious laugh. 'But don't speak too loud.'

'You must come back,' repeated Sally breathlessly.

'Why? Anything happened?'

'No, but…'

'You mean nobody's discovered?'

'Nobody, but…'

'Then I'm not coming back.'

'Oh…'

'Listen!' Philippa went on interrupting. 'If you've got away with it overnight and this morning, then it's okay by me, as they say in America, and I'm *not* coming back.'

'But I can't go on!' cried Sally frantically.

'Why not?'

'It's too much of a strain, and oh, I hate it all and…'

'Be quiet. Just listen to me. You promised you'd do this and give me my holiday and you can't back out on me now.'

Sally started to remonstrate but her cousin gave her no opportunity.

'Pull yourself together, you little idiot, and carry on as you have been doing. You seem to have been a great success so far, so why throw in the sponge now? We've had it all out. You know why I need this change, and it's too dangerous for us to discuss it on the phone. Just carry on till I come back.'

'No … wait…!' Sally was quite white under her tan and her hands were shaking.

'My dear child, I repeat that I can't come back now. I'm at Dover, anyhow.'

'Dover!' echoed Sally in dismay.

'Yes, I've changed my mind about Ireland.

I'm going to Paris.'

'Oh, no, please, you can't go all that way away...'

'It's all arranged and I'm going. Write to me at the Hotel Crillon. Get the bank to wire me that money that I want to Miss Maxwell. I've drawn out the whole of my deposit at the bank so if you want to draw any money for yourself you'll have to get *him* to give you some. You can manage it. You've got the signature to copy. Good-bye. And *don't* forget the money I want, otherwise I shall starve in Paris. I'm going to join a married cousin...' the lie came glibly... 'But I've got to have cash. No ... don't argue ... it would be too cruel of you to back out on me now ... and on Martin...'

'Yes, but...'

'Good-bye!' interrupted Philippa. 'And keep going ... just for a month!'

'Listen, please!'

There was a click the other end.

'Hullo! Hullo!' said Sally frantically.

And then came the droning tone of the automatic telephone. Sally replaced the instrument on its stand. Her heart was thumping and now her cheeks were hot with anger. Philippa had no right to do this. Why should she force this thing on her? And how dared she leave the country ... in case anything happened!

Weakly, Sally collapsed into a chair and sat

99

there staring in front of her, her brows knit, her thoughts confused. This was largely her own fault, of course. She should never have consented to such a mad arrangement! And in a way, Phil was justified in saying that she could not back out now. It *was* too late.

Gradually the anger, the chaotic excitement, died. Sally's thoughts turned to the man downstairs. *'It would be too cruel of you to back out on Martin...'* Phil had said. Yes, true enough. And if Phil was leaving the country, she, Sally, could scarcely 'down tools' and leave Martin in the lurch. She must go on playing her part and playing it to the best of her ability. For if he were to discover the truth, not only would he be horrified, but it would break his heart ... if Philippa had not already broken it ... to think that she could so easily leave him and practise this deception upon him.

Sally put a hand to her forehead in a bewildered way. Either it was very hot and close this September morning, or it was just her state of mind which made her feel stifled. She must get out into the fresh air now that Philippa's call had come.

Sally walked into the bedroom, combed her fair shining hair, put on a wide-brimmed hat which Vera had put out for her, picked up bag and delicate suède gloves, and walked downstairs.

This was not at all what she had meant

should happen. She had made up her mind to leave Harley Street this morning. She could scarcely believe that she must remain here, play this incredible part for a whole month.

Sally faced the fact that she would be standing on the brink of disaster every day, if not every hour, until Philippa came back. At any moment she might give herself away or be detected. It would surely be impossible that she should remain here for so long, in constant companionship with Martin, and not be found out. Even though her likeness to her cousin was so rare, so amazing, assuredly a man must know his own wife? Eventually he must find out that she, Sally, was just a substitute. Well, *if* and when that moment came, heaven help them all! Martin might forgive his wife, but he would scarcely forgive *her*. Did that matter? Was he of any real importance in her life? Couldn't she, as Philippa had suggested, just look upon it as an amusing interlude, an interesting experiment, and take what fun she could get out of it. It could do no ultimate harm.

Outside the library door, Sally paused and her heart began to pound again. In there lay a man who was relying on her, who had just told her that he would make a special effort to get well so that he could go out with her. And it *did* matter what he thought. It seemed to matter quite a lot how much he suffered, too. He had been through so much already. She wanted to help, to protect him from further pain. She felt partly responsible for him now. Philippa had gone and left her with that responsibility.

She remembered what Philippa had said about money. That was going to be the most hateful and difficult part of all. All her life Sally had shrunk from asking for things. When she was still in her teens she had tried to be economical, to do without things rather than ask her father to spend the money which he could ill afford.

Martin Frome was a rich man. Philippa had said that he could afford most things. But Sally could scarcely bear the thought of making any demands upon him now. On the other hand she would have to. Philippa needed money at once. She, Sally, must send it. And Philippa needed at least a hundred pounds right away, she had said:

'Martin won't turn a hair if you tell him that you're overdrawn and that you want another hundred … just pat his hand and ask nicely.'

Sally felt a trifle sick at the memory of those words. *'Pat his hand and ask nicely!'* … That was how Philippa got her way. Despicable! And Martin still loved her blindly enough to concede, and never resent it.

It was a thing that must be done, and the sooner the better, Sally told herself. But she was fiercely reluctant. All her instincts revolted from it. She supposed that she must consider it the penalty for taking part in this deception of Martin.

With a heavy heart Sally opened the library door and walked in.

6

Leaning over the rails of a Channel steamer, this warm tranquil day of September, Martin Frome's real wife laughed and talked in the highest spirits to the man beside her. A slim ivory-skinned man with sleek black hair, and melting almond eyes, and that unmistakable touch of the Spaniard about him. Ivor Lexon's mother had been Andalusian.

'Isn't this superb, Ivor?' Philippa said for the hundredth time as the boat carried her nearer the shores of France.

He smiled with a genuine appreciation of the *soignée* and beautiful young woman in her tweed cape and the black beret on the side of her fair, well-groomed head. He was madly in love with Philippa Frome. More madly than he had been with anybody. And the whole unusual nature of this illicit romance appealed to his jaded instincts which were in need of stimulation. It wasn't often that one could take a month in Paris with an attractive woman at somebody else's expense, and with no fear of being made a co-respondent.

'It's incredible,' he said, and drew her arm tightly to his side. 'You beautiful thing!' he added in that husky undertone which had made a dozen women in London risk their reputations for his sake.

'Nothing to worry about,' she said dreamily. 'No interruptions, no having to rush home to play the ministering angel, no having to hide in corners in hotels because somebody we know may see us. Just you and I – and heaven! Of course, we won't stay at the Crillon. We'll wander about. But that must be my headquarters for mail.'

'It shall all be as you wish, my sweet. I suppose I'm a cad to let you do this, in case it's ever discovered, but, you know how I feel...' He pressed her closer to his side... 'Oh, I can't live unless I breathe the air that you breathe ... see you .. yes, I ask nothing more than to look at you ... you're so beautiful!'

Philippa gave a satisfied little sigh. Ivor was really a charming lover. If one's husband said things like that they fell so flat, became so boring. But with Ivor it was all exciting, intriguing …. the two things which were the breath of life to Philippa Frome.

'Darling Ivor, I shan't allow you only to look at me. Why, dar-*ling!*'

He immediately seized her hand and pressed a passionate kiss into the fragrant palm.

'Divine lady!'

'Sally tried to get out of it when I phoned her at Dover, but I wasn't going to allow that,' added Philippa.

'This Sally,' said Ivor Lexon, shaking his head, 'is it possible that she can be so like you ... that there can be any other woman in the world so beautiful?'

Philippa shrugged her shoulders.

'Of course there are subtle differences. I mean, *you* might notice...'

'But not the husband?'

'Well, you see, my dear, we aren't on those terms nowadays!'

'Ah!' said Ivor, nodding his head sagely.

Delicately Philippa passed that over.

'And, of course, Martin is a sick man and lies in a half-darkened room and I don't suppose there'll be any difference by the time I get back. Sally is really remarkably like me so far as features and colouring go. It wouldn't enter Martin's head, for instance, to examine her hands and see whether our nails were precisely the same shape, or notice that she had a tiny mole beside the ear which I haven't got. It would be different if one was *looking* for such details.'

'Or if, like me, Martin knew and adored every hair of your glorious head,' murmured Ivor passionately.

'I daresay he might have done so when we were first married,' said Philippa, yawning. 'But not nowadays. I daresay Martin's as fed up with me as I am with him, if the truth were known. I only wish to God you were in the position to take me away for good and all.'

'God, if only I were!'

'Well, we must be thankful for this month.'

'Devoutly, my angel.'

'Funny, isn't it, that Sally should have come along at the psychological moment? No relations, nobody in the world to worry about, except a fiancé in South Africa who appears to be pretty lukewarm about her.'

'If he's lukewarm, then this Sally doesn't resemble *you!*' said Ivor.

Philippa Frome gave a little gurgle of laughter.

'Let's go and have a cocktail.'

'And, by the way, if your cousin makes a blunder or Martin discovers the truth, you're quite certain you won't suffer?'

'So sweet of you to worry about me,' drawled Philippa, 'but you needn't worry. I'll manage Martin if he finds out. And, anyhow, he'll never know about you and me. I've got a cousin living in Paris and I can square her. She'll be my alibi, in case of necessity.'

'And Cousin Sally is to be trusted?'

'Completely. She's most virtuous. She's really only doing this because she thinks she's saving a calamity and she's sorry for Martin.'

'I'm sorry for the poor devil, too. But I'm sorrier for myself, because you're his wife and not mine.'

With that remark to flavour the cocktail, Ivor Lexon took Philippa's arm and led her to the bar.

And it was at this precise moment that Sally approached Martin and made her request for a hundred pounds. She tried to make it as she imagined her cousin would have done, lightly, and without remorse. But she felt horribly guilty and ashamed. She was going to ask for this money in cash. She really could not face Philippa's bank before she had practised that signature a bit more often. That amounted to forgery. On the other hand, it could scarcely be called *forging* when Philippa had given her the right! It was all complicated and abhorrent to Sally with her naturally honest mind.

Martin received the request for money without any visible sign of annoyance. He was not annoyed because he had to part with the money. Rather, he was disappointed in the girl whom he thought his wife. Had he been a fool, after all, to think that she was changing? Wasn't this what he had anticipated … a show of sweetness on Phil's part before 'asking for more'?

'Certainly you can have a hundred pounds, darling,' he told her. 'But how naughty of you to be overdrawn already. What have you been spending it all on?'

Sally turned a scarlet face away from him.

'Oh, lots of things.'

'Well, be a little temperate, my sweet. I don't want to be mean, but it doesn't look as though I'm going to swell our income by my earnings in future. Stenning was most optimistic just now, but it may be the dickens of a time before I can get back to work. Of course we've got plenty, but it's a big house to keep up and...'

'Oh, please!' interrupted Sally, feeling she could bear no more. 'I – I'll try to be careful.'

Martin's thin face lit up with his humorous smile.

'Spoiled baby.'

Sally gritted her teeth. Then, perforce, made the second request that the money should be paid in cash, because she had so many small bills to settle.

'Get Miss Swithen to settle them for you,' said Martin.

Sally gulped. Miss Swithen was Martin's secretary. She remembered that. She stammered on:

'I – I think I'd rather do it myself.'

Martin put his tongue in his cheek. What was his Philippa up to now, he wondered. And suddenly he saw that she was blushing. That astonished him. Philippa very rarely changed colour except when she was angry. He teased her.

'Why the pink cheeks, dearest? What's on

109

your little conscience?'

Sally felt that she would scream in a moment. She spoke quite curtly in consequence.

'Nothing at all.'

And it was so like Philippa to snap that Martin felt very much at home with her and sighed to himself. Where was the tender and gentle Phil of whom he had been thinking and dreaming half the long morning chained to his couch, unutterably weary, and with a brain so active that it was positive torment not to be able to get up and go about his job.

'Never mind, Phil,' he said. 'I didn't mean to upset you. Have the money in cash, by all means. Tell Miss Swithen when she comes this afternoon to write the cheque and bring it to me, and then she can cash it before three and give it to you if you want it urgently. And if you're as low in funds as all that, darling, I'd better pay another hundred into the bank for you.'

Sally looked at him speechlessly. She felt choked. He was so incredibly good and generous and everything that a woman could want in a man! Philippa must be crazy not to appreciate him, ill or well. And that other hundred would be a godsend, because after she wired Philippa the money, she would want a little pocket money to keep up appearances.

Martin held out a hand.

'Still angry?'

Sally seized the hand and burst out:

'No, no, of course not! You're a dear … it's sweet of you… I think you're frightfully good…'

That made him blink. It was a change from Philippa's usual cold and careless: 'Thanks, Martin.'

Sally added hastily:

'And what about the drive? What did Dr Stenning say?'

'Perhaps next week. He wants me to lie quiet to-day, and to-morrow when my masseur comes I'm going to put my feet on the ground. Think of that, Phil! It'll be mighty good to feel the floor again.'

'It'll be fine!' she exclaimed.

His bright, tired eyes travelled over her. He was not noticing detail particularly. He was just drinking in the fair beauty of the slim figure in grey, as a whole. But Sally, conscious of his gaze, dropped his hand and turned from him. It almost hurt to hear his voice follow her.

'Must you go?'

'I'll come back. After lunch…'

'Oh no, I don't want to be a selfish swine, darling. You'll have some engagement. I shall sleep a bit, and I'm going to dictate one or two letters to Swithen. Don't worry about me.'

Sally knew perfectly well that he didn't

111

sleep, couldn't. She had spoken to Watson for a few minutes this morning and he had told her that the doctor's chief trouble at the moment was that he could not sleep and he would not be doped. She could imagine how long, how tedious were the hours which he had to live through, after leading his full and interesting life.

At the door she turned back to him and smiled.

'I insist on having tea with you, Martin.'

And she was well rewarded by his expression when he said:

'*Angel!*'

She went upstairs and cried a little, by herself.

7

The week that followed was exciting for Sally, to say nothing of chaotic.

It was only when she was in bed at night that she could really say that she was at peace. Every hour of the daytime was fraught with anxiety, spoiling the pleasure which might otherwise have been hers. For a pleasure it was, undoubtedly, to live in the Fromes' lovely house and partake of some of the thrills which had never before been Sally's, although to Philippa this was just everyday existence.

Lovely in a purely sensuous fashion to wallow in luxury, good servants, wonderful food, gorgeous clothes, cars, and to be surrounded by so many things of beauty. Most of the pictures, books and exquisite furniture and appointments, Sally discovered, Martin had collected or inherited from his father. He had the true artistic appreciation. Philippa's taste was slightly more flamboyant. Really the room that Sally liked least was the ultra-modern boudoir. But she revelled in the books and music which were hers to enjoy down in that library ... the room that Philippa had found so gloomy! And she was never tired of wandering around the long handsome drawing-room which contained some particularly fine paintings and collectors' china.

She had soon discovered that Martin was as much an artist in his mind as a surgeon. He seemed to her to have unlimited intelligence, a far-reaching mind and understanding which appealed to her vastly.

Sally was not clever. She did not pretend to be. But she had the receptive type of mind and she was hungry for knowledge, ready to absorb anything that Martin could teach her. Obviously, Philippa had never wanted to be taught and had never really bothered to explore the depths of her husband's learning or sharpen her own wits on his intellect. She was just a lovely sensualist, greedy for admiration; pretty froth on the champagne of life.

Part of Sally's difficulty was the endeavour to pour herself into that mould which was really entirely unsuited to her temperament. And whenever she forgot herself so far as to question Martin about things which interested her, she had to pull herself up and keep silence because he expressed so much surprise at what he thought her unusual curiosity.

She was quite sure that living with her day by day he must eventually discover that she was not Philippa. And it was this constant state of panic which tried her nerves so sorely and spoilt her happiness.

Every hour a pitfall presented itself ready for her to fall into. There were so many things she could not know, so many habits that Philippa had of which she was ignorant, so much that she dared not do, so many of Philippa's friends whom she dared not meet, and yet must eventually come up against.

There was the trouble of Philippa's small car. Sally could not drive. She had never been in a position to afford a car. Philippa was an experienced driver. Sally had to pretend that the weather was so hot that it tired her to drive herself about town. Thus she allowed Smith to take her everywhere in the big Daimler.

Very nice it was to sit back in that smooth gliding limousine, when most of her life had been spent in waiting for crowded buses, and hanging on to straps in the tube! Oh, yes, life was made easy for women like Philippa Frome, thought Sally. Yet how unhappy she was! So unhappy that she had not been able to bear her existence and had rushed away!

The more that Sally saw of Martin Frome the more deeply he attracted her. She felt that it would have been easy to sit always at the feet of such a man. His present physical disabilities meant nothing. She liked to talk to him, do little things for him. Philippa had not been far wrong in her judgement of Sally, in guessing that she would glory in her 'job'.

Sally grew to like it not merely because she had pitied Martin, but because she admired him. She felt that it would be an insult to offer pity to a man with such a wonderful character, and such a fine and generous soul.

She grew used to lying, almost past blushing, because one grows used to anything. But she could never accustom herself to the thought that she was practising such deception upon Martin.

It seemed mean, although she knew that she was doing nothing mean to him, really. She was helping him. He said so, never failed to tell her how much she helped. He was growing better. He had astonished his medical advisers by the sudden change in his progress, the rapidity with which he was gaining new health and strength.

'Philippa' seemed to want him to get better quickly, and it was for her he exerted every effort, mental and physical. Science, medicine, surgery, could achieve much, but there was so much more that will-power could do in a case like this. Sally, knowing that she inspired him, tried to remember that fact whenever conscience stabbed her guiltily.

If only she could have been – just Sally! How wonderful to let herself go and not have to guard her tongue, or think carefully before every little action or speech. And what a relief it would be to talk to Martin – as Sally. She grew positively sick of having to curb all her most natural instincts in order to ape Philippa … Philippa the egotist, the empty-headed, the flint-hearted! She could look like Philippa, but never, never, would she *be* Philippa. That was impossible.

She collected her South African mail from the boarding-house in Bayswater. Rex was still writing there, of course.

His last letter had been typical of him. Not very long. He never expressed himself in many words. Just short, breezy, giving her bits of news about his work and his family, and with little of the passion and longing which she had always tried futilely to find in his letters.

Since her engagement Sally had made up her mind that Rex could never be a lover in the poetic sense, but that it was 'all there', and must be taken for granted. Yet how difficult to feel her pulses stir and her heart throb at such a paragraph as the last one in his most recent epistle:

'Hope you're all right, old girl. Must be mouldy for you without the gov'nor and I daresay you're a bit lonely. Would give anything to have you out here, but money's so tight. There are no jobs going, so hang on. We must look forward to the great day, next year. All my love, Sally darling.

'Yours ever,
'REX.'

Sally read and re-read those words, not because they were inspiring, but because she *wanted* them to mean so much more than they really did ... to enthuse into them some of her own sensitive loving and tenderness. But she failed dismally. And she was miserable because she felt that she was failing Rex in not being satisfied with what he said or did.

He sent her *'all his love'*. What more could he do? Nothing. And he looked forward to *'the great day'*. She couldn't complain. It was just a rather uninspired and reticent letter written by a typical everyday man. There weren't many who indulged in *grandes passions* or could pen flaming, thrilling love letters. She was just a romantic little idiot and Rex would be the first to tell her so.

She ought to be satisfied with his love. It had contented her when she had first met and fallen in love with him. Why, why had everything altered? The answer in her own heart reproached Sally because she felt that it was she, rather than Rex, who had altered. She had rushed into an engagement when she had been most bored and tired of her prosaic existence at home and the young man from South Africa had seemed to open the gates of another and more thrilling life.

In other words she had been infatuated with Rex. But after that trip to South Africa and back she had not felt so certain of herself. She had ceased to invest him with those qualities which he did not possess and had just found him an ordinary, and occasionally, quite irritating, young man. A disappointing lover, who in mundane fashion, was willing to put up with a protracted engagement and very little romance. And if he was like this before marriage, what would he be like afterwards? That was the thought that frightened Sally now and made her feel that she had been mad ever to dedicate the rest of her life to Rex or imagine that she would fulfil her true destiny as his wife.

There was something more than disappointment and disillusion in this matter too. She had to admit *that* to herself during the many long hours which she spent in puzzling and trying to work things out.

Her introduction to Martin Frome and this strangely intimate life which she led with him in Philippa's place had altered her whole outlook. *He* had unconsciously altered it and no matter how much she tried to avoid doing so, she inevitably drew comparisons between Martin and Rex. Martin was a man to be adored, and she knew she could never adore Rex in the literal sense of the word, no matter how fond she was of him. And Martin's love for Philippa was the kind of love which she, Sally, had always wanted. Therein lay another, deeper explanation of her changed feelings and the present unhappy disorder of her mind.

It was not altogether her fault. Yet she did not excuse herself. Rex had been found wanting. He had responded to her enthusiastic young love in lukewarm fashion. In a measure he had failed her. Yet even that thought did not make Sally feel that she was to be excused for failing him.

She worried desperately over the affair and wrote an even more than usually loving letter to him, trying to put this engagement back on its old high plane in her mind. But even while she did so it was with a sinking sensation in her heart and the knowledge that once love has fallen from its pedestal it breaks in so many pieces that it can never be really mended or elevated again.

So it could not truly be said that Sally was enjoying her masquerade.

On the other hand, Philippa appeared to be happy. Sally had wired her the hundred pounds and had received from Paris just the short reply: *'Thanks. Having glorious holiday. – Maxwell.'*

What Philippa was really doing in Paris as 'Miss Maxwell', Sally didn't bother to think. She had so much to do her end, she could not concern herself very vastly with Philippa's movements.

She felt that she was now fairly safe with the staff. They had all accepted her. And even

Denham, who had seen the cousin 'Miss Browning' on that day when she had arrived, had apparently thought no more about it and never suspected an exchange of identities. The one or two appointments which Sally kept passed off without catastrophe.

She had thought it too dangerous to cancel every engagement and stay too much with Martin, although her whole inclinations were in that direction. She liked parties, but not the kind in which Philippa indulged. These society functions seemed to Sally too highly artificial and futile. Besides it gave her so much more pleasure to sit with Martin and see that contented look which never failed to come into his eyes when he was in her company.

Yesterday she had gone to a big cocktail party given by a theatrical celebrity and found herself accosted from all sides by people who, of course, she had never seen in her life before. But she managed to pull it off by replying to the 'Hello, darling,' or 'Hello, Phil,' with a gay smile and murmured greeting. Nobody had any devastating questions to ask, nor seemed to indulge in anything but idle chatter to which she could easily respond.

There was one awkward moment. A red-haired girl, with very red lips and lashes thick with mascara, wearing grey chiffon, and whom everybody called 'Toni' clutched her arm and said:

'Phil, darling, don't forget to send me that book you promised. Can I have it by to-night?'

Sally, quite ignorant, was for a moment flummoxed, and then thought it best to be sincere.

'To tell you the truth I've forgotten the name of it,' she replied.

Toni gave her an amazed stare and said:

'*Darl*ing, then your brain must be going. We spent the entire evening discussing it. Don't you remember?'

'I remember the discussion, but not the book,' murmured Sally.

Toni tapped her forehead, significantly, suggested that 'Phil should see a brain specialist,' and added:

'Why, it was that new book which has been banned. *Drink Deep*... You said you'd bought a copy from the library before it was withdrawn and I'm dying to read it. And don't forget to underline those pieces we talked about.'

Sally murmured a promise and moved away, thoroughly embarrassed. She was beginning to know Cousin Phil well. And she could not help being contemptuous of her. Sally was no prude, but it would never have entered her head to rush for a banned book or underline the most absorbing pieces. She told herself that 'Toni' would get that book as it was. Sally did not even intend to read it. And then the next thing she had to do was to find out *who Toni was!* That was difficult. But eventually Sally found herself chatting to a stranger who had, apparently, never met Philippa before. The stranger knew Toni and pointed her out as a 'Mrs Arnmouth'.

After that it did not take long for Sally to discover that Toni Arnmouth had been mixed up recently in a somewhat notorious divorce case. And she was one of Philippa's intimate friends! Sally wondered how good that could be for Martin's reputation.

She found the book in her boudoir and sent it to Mrs Arnmouth minus an accompanying note. That was one thing she could *not* do: write Philippa's letters for her!

Sometimes in the midst of such harassing moments Sally thought of her cousin with exceeding irritation and wondered if she ever gave a thought to them all here; she appeared to be just amusing herself in Paris and not bothering about anybody else. True, she had sent the key of her jewel case. She had posted that from Dover in a registered envelope. But she answered neither of the long letters which Sally wrote. Obviously she meant to ignore any protests that Sally made to the effect that she 'could not go on'. Philippa meant her to go on so that she could pursue her own selfish course. A ruthless egotist, Philippa.

And Sally carried on more for Martin's sake than anybody else's.

Then came the day when Martin set foot to the ground for the first time since his accident.

It was on a Monday morning. Harold Stenning, the specialist, was present. Sally received an urgent message from Martin to go down to the library at once.

She opened the door with some trepidation, wondering if something was wrong. She saw Martin standing up, supported on one side by Watson, and on the other by a big curly-headed man whom she realised was Dr Stenning, because she had seen his Lanchester drive up Harley Street and stop at their door.

Then she concentrated on Martin. It was odd to see him standing upright like that. She had never known him except on his couch. She was struck first of all by his height. He was quite tall and so much too thin. The blue silk dressing-gown hung on a wasted frame. But his eyes were shining and his face radiated happiness.

'Phil!' he cried as she entered. 'Why, Phil, look, I can really stand. And I can walk a few steps. Look!'

'Oh, Martin, how lovely. Do go on!' she said.

Like a pathetic, unsteady child learning to walk, Martin put one foot before the other and, with the help of the two men, made a movement into the middle of the room.

'It's good to see it, sir,' little Watson was saying with moisture in his eyes.

Harold Stenning put an arm round Martin's waist.

'No more to-day, old chap. Back to your couch.'

'What did you think of that, Phil?' cried Martin.

She smiled at him.

'Why, it's marvellous ... wonderful, Martin!' she said.

Stenning eyed her suspiciously. There was no woman in London whom he more cordially disliked than Philippa Frome. And that was possibly because there was no man in his profession whom he liked and admired more than Martin. He and Martin were contemporaries and had been at Bart's together. He considered Martin not only one of the most able of the younger surgeons in town but one of the nicest fellows he had ever met. Right from the start he had been gloomy about Martin's marriage. Stenning was a confirmed bachelor and beauty in a woman appealed to him only in an aesthetic sense. In that sense he was bound to admit that Philippa was good to look upon. But he despised her. He resented the poor way in which she returned Martin's devotion and he had been in a state of quiet indignation about her ever since Martin's accident. She had been so incredibly indifferent, even callous, and Stenning had known all along that nobody could help Martin more than his wife if she chose to give him that *élan* for existence at the present time.

He was somewhat surprised this morning when he regarded the slender, lovely figure and saw that she was expressing real pleasure at the sight of Martin's progress.

'Simply marvellous, Martin' she repeated. 'But you mustn't overdo it. Do go back to your couch now, as Dr Stenning says.'

'Every day I shall be able to do a bit more,' Martin said.

He was breathless. His thick brown hair was damp with perspiration, but he was a happy man, triumphant, all the more so because Philippa, so he imagined, smiled her appreciation.

Stenning helped his patient back to a comfortable position on the couch. He thought:

'Wonder what's happened to Mrs Martin. She's a bit more human to-day!'

He was still more surprised when Sally plied him with questions about Martin.

How rapid would the progress be? When would he be able to walk alone? How much must he do every day without hurting himself? When could he go out for a drive?

'Damn it,' Stenning reflected, 'I've never seen such a change in anybody. You'd never think that it was the same person. Usually she shows as much interest in him as a sick cat! Hanged if I can understand women. They're as changeable as the devil.'

He told Sally what she wanted to know. Martin must go very easy at first. He could take a few steps more every morning and keep on with the massage and exercises and there seemed every chance of the injured nerves in the right leg and hip recovering almost completely.

'And the drive?' asked Sally.

'Oh, I see no reason why he shouldn't go out for a bit to-morrow, if it's fine,' Stenning told her.

Sally turned to Martin.

'Isn't that grand!'

He looked up at her with that wide, boyish grin which she knew by now was indicative of happiness.

'Grand!' he echoed. 'And are you going to be bored driving me, sweet?'

'Oh, I don't think I shall drive you,' she said self-consciously. 'It will be better if I come with you in the Daimler and let Smith do the driving.'

'But I like being driven by you,' he persisted.

Sally's heart sank. But Harold Stenning unwittingly came to her rescue. Personally he had no belief in women as drivers.

'I think the bigger car would be better.

Less jolting and movement and the rest of it,' he murmured.

'Oh, all right,' said Martin, sighed and settled himself on his cushions. 'I'm quite exhausted by that effort,' he added.

'Are you sure you're all right?' came from Sally anxiously.

'You bet I am. And as impatient for that drive to-morrow as a thirsty man for a drink. I don't seem to have seen anything but four walls around me for the deuce of a time.'

'The drive will be wonderful for you,' she said.

'*You're* wonderful for me,' he whispered as Stenning crossed the room to pick up his case.

Sally felt suddenly, absurdly elated. She was not sorry for Martin any more. But just happy because she was making him happy. And when he held out a hand for a surreptitious squeeze, she responded to it.

Martin wondered what he had done to be so favoured by the gods. For days now his Phil had been kind and soft and charming. He was never done marvelling at the change in her. He could even forget the fact that she had asked for money. At least she was repaying him a thousandfold. She was doing everything she could to help him now. All the old wild love for her was crowding back into his heart, stronger, more intense than it had ever been. But still he was afraid to show her too much of what he felt ... terrified lest at a touch this present dream would be shattered. He felt that at all costs Phil must be kept in her present mood. It was too good to miss, too sweet to lose, even though the ache of passionate desire for her persisted in him, unsatisfied.

Her kindness and her companionship meant so much more than anything and he felt that he must ask no more.

The morning was a full one and for Martin, anyhow, one of the most cheerful he had known since his accident. Both his physician and his oculist were optimistic.

Dacre Cheniston came along just before lunch to examine his eyes and passed a favourable verdict. He could have a little more light now in the room and although for a while he must wear smoked glasses when he went out, he would soon be able to do without them altogether.

Sally saw that she was expected to greet Martin's medical advisers as though she knew them well, so she held out a hand to Mr Cheniston when he arrived. She thought that he resembled Martin a little. Perhaps it was that touch of sadness in the face. Later she learned Cheniston's interesting history and how he had once been struck off the medical register in error, through the wilful and wicked lies of a society girl who had been rejected by him and trumped up evidence against his morality.

He had been reinstated and had since been a tremendous success in his job. Sally immediately liked him, although she found his manner a little cold and distant. But it was apparent to her that none of these medical men liked Philippa and Sally was sensitive enough to understand why.

It was a little awkward for her when Martin said:

'Dacre tells me his wife's out in the car. Run out and say a word to her, Phil. She apparently won't come in.'

'Please don't trouble, Mrs Frome,' Cheniston said a trifle swiftly. 'My wife always brings a book to read. She likes to come with me on my rounds on Monday mornings. She isn't a bit bored.'

And he said that mainly because he knew that his wife could not bear Mrs Frome. But Sally, feeling that it was her duty to go, walked out to the oculist's car.

She was not quite sure on what terms. Philippa was with Mrs Cheniston, and greeted her with some embarrassment. But the next moment she was almost forgetting to be Philippa and was just Sally. Jan Cheniston struck her as being one of the sweetest women she had ever seen. She, too, had known tragedy,. It was written in those large dark eyes of hers, but her smile was sweet and happy and she was quite friendly.

'How is Mr Frome?'

'Oh, much better to-day.'

'That's good. Dacre will be so glad.'

'It was wonderful to see him walk this morning,' said Sally.

Jan Cheniston came nearer to liking Martin's wife this morning than she had ever done. Usually she shared the general opinion in the medical profession, that Martin's wife was beautiful but 'impossible'. And as a rule, Philippa treated Jan Cheniston with faint disdain ... because Jan was 'the perfect wife and mother' and, to Philippa, dull in consequence.

Sally was sympathetic and charming this morning, however, and the two women chatted quite pleasantly for a few moments and Sally appeared to make no mistakes. Conservation was too non-committal.

As the Cheniston's car drove away from Harley Street, Jan said:

'I've never known her so nice, have you, Dacre?'

'No. She seems to have softened considerably. I don't know why.'

'I've always felt so sorry for Martin Frome.'

Dacre Cheniston glanced at his wife and as he swung the car round into Wigmore Street, picked up her hand and dropped a kiss on it.

'I've always been sorry for anybody who

hasn't a wife like you, Jan.'

'Outrageous,' she said, 'to flirt with your wife when you've been married more than two years!'

'Two centuries won't be long enough for me,' was Dacre Cheniston's reply.

And nobody listening to these two or looking at them this morning would have guessed that tragedy had laid a finger upon both of them and that they had once been so near lifelong separation.

Back in the Frome's library, Martin was talking to Sally.

'How's Mrs Dacre?'

'She seems well. She really has got wonderful eyes!' Sally burst out impulsively.

Martin gave her a puzzled look.

Phil had always shown faint contempt for Jan Cheniston. There had been moments lately when Martin had been frankly bewildered by one or two things that Phil had said, one or two most perplexing changes in her attitude toward people and things. But he did no more than puzzle. There seemed no answer to the problem, and no cause for complaint as the changes were all for the better.

'I've always admired her,' he said. 'Look how she stuck to Cheniston over that Royter case.'

Here Sally kept silence. She had not the slightest idea what the Royter case was about. Then Martin added:

'Did you ask after the baby?'

'I – I forgot,' stammered Sally.

That was like Philippa. She had never been interested in children. Martin looked at the beloved painting in front of his couch and a faint sigh escaped him. How perfect it would have been if Phil had given him a child ... a boy like that little chap of the Chenistons' to whom he was godfather.

'By the way, Phil,' he said turning to Sally again, 'it's that kid's birthday in a week or so. October 4th, isn't it? Be an angel and buy something for me. I must do my duty as a godparent.'

Sally thanked her lucky stars he had added that piece of information so that now she knew where she was. She showed such interest in what the present should be that Martin was puzzled anew.

He gave a somewhat wry smile.

'Darling, don't be *too* much of a martyr for my sake.'

Sally looked indignant.

'Why?'

'Well, you know you loathe babies, and you're not in the least interested in the Chenistons'. I'm sure you don't want to hunt for hours round the shops for the kid's present.'

Sally bit her lip.

'Oh lord,' she thought, '*I* loathe babies!

When I just *adore* them! This really is a hopeless situation.'

'Don't bore yourself, darling,' added Martin. 'Just tell Harrods toy department to send off something suitable.'

'But it isn't old enough for a toy yet if it's only a year!' broke out Sally.

'Fancy you knowing that!'

She sat silent, absurdly annoyed.

8

Another week went by. Seven more days of difficulty for Sally, although in a way each day was growing less difficult because with every twenty-four hours that went by, she grew more accustomed to her rôle as Philippa Frome.

Martin's progress was wonderful. At the end of that second week he could walk on two sticks the full length of the library and he went out with her for a drive every morning.

Those drives were a great success. They went no further than the parks but Martin, with smoked glasses over his eyes, revelled in the sunshine and being able to be out in the fresh air again. His childlike pleasure in everything almost made Sally weep. His pleasure in her, personally, was limitless. He had ceased to be surprised because she was nice to him. He just accepted her change of demeanour gladly and with gratitude and never ceased to show the latter in a dozen different ways.

Every morning now, a bunch of flowers, something choice and exquisite, arrived for Philippa's boudoir with a little card from Martin. And he had sent for a new ring for her, an aquamarine set in platinum. It looked like blue ice-water, very lovely on Sally's slim, sun-browned finger.

She protested when she received the ring.

'I – I've so many jewels already,' she stammered.

But Martin pressed the gift upon her and told her that he wanted her to have it just 'because she had been so sweet'.

And this was the wonderful husband who bored Philippa! Sally felt that never in a thousand years would she understand her cousin's attitude toward Martin.

Much more than the ring did she treasure the daily bouquet. That ring was Philippa's, would be left behind in the jewel case with all the other rings. But the flowers, she felt, were hers. Long before the real Philippa returned they would be withered.

Sally brooded over her flowers, not only because they were beautiful but for sentimental reasons. She had to confess that sentiment played a large part in her present association with Martin. Admiration for him was developing, daily, hourly, into something more individual, more *intimate*. She was growing personally, deeply attached to this man who was her cousin's husband. His devotion was no longer an embarrassment. In a curious way, it was becoming a necessity to her. She would have felt lost without it.

He made things so easy by not demanding

too much. There were times when she felt that she was mean to take all that he gave and return so little. Had she been his wife she would so gladly have given everything. That was a thought which disturbed her considerably.

Having played the part of Martin's wife for a fortnight she knew she wanted to go on playing it for ever!

Sally grew afraid. To begin with, she knew that she would *have* to relinquish the part in a fortnight's time, and to end with, she was pledged to somebody else. To Rex.

She was definite in her feelings about Rex now, and therein lay more trouble. She was no longer in love with him. To herself she could not even pretend to be. She wrote to him with the utmost difficulty, feeling that every word of love was forced and insincere and she was playing a mean double part. She could no longer even compare him in her mind with Martin. Martin Frome was outstanding. The very incarnation of any dreams of love which she had dreamt when she was a young girl. She loved him. Yes, that was indisputable. All that she did for him now sprang not from pity, but from love for him.

Philippa had replied to no letters. But she wired for more money, and this time Sally had not felt able to make the demand upon Martin. It would have caused her too much shame and distress. She just drew out the hundred pounds that had been placed to her credit as pocket money and sent it to Philippa. So far as she, Sally, was concerned, she was content to do without any pocket money. She went nowhere, did nothing that could make her spend money.

She devoted more and more of her time to Martin and now the staff in the Harley Street house had ceased to shrug shoulders and sneer. Even Watson was converted, if secretly jealous. It seemed pretty apparent that 'her ladyship' had turned over a new leaf and the servants grew used to seeing their mistress in the doctor's company.

But one or two people did not get used to it. For one, Toni Arnmouth, who was Philippa's bosom friend, continually pestered Sally with calls and messages. On receiving no success, Toni started to abuse her.

'You are doing too much of this devoted wife business nowadays,' she said to Sally when at last she got her on the telephone one day. 'I think you might spare a little time for me. After all, I was a damn good friend to you when you first fell for Ivor. Perhaps it's because you just don't need to make use of my flat any more.'

Sally, scarlet to the roots of her hair, and loathing the inference of this remark, answered Toni shortly. Whereupon Toni said:

'It's not my fault, anyhow, if Ivor's flitted to Paris with some other female. You ought to know how to keep a lover, my dear! However, come to my roulette party to-morrow and show there's no ill-feeling.'

'I'm sorry I can't.'

'Sitting with the husband?' sneered Toni.

'Yes,' said Sally, and hung up the receiver.

That was a shock. The brief quarrel with Mrs Arnmouth had opened Sally's eyes to one outstanding fact. Philippa had a lover ... Ivor Lexon, of course. Martin had asked once or twice where 'Ivor' was. It must be the same one. *And he had gone to Paris.* Much as Sally disliked jumping to hasty conclusions, this one stared her in the face.

She felt a trifle sick as she sat down and brooded after the conversation with Toni Arnmouth. Toni openly called Ivor Lexon 'a lover'. And Philippa had been mad to get away, not because she needed a holiday, but because she wanted...

Sally allowed her imagination to run no further. It was too horrible. She, Sally, had unwittingly been a party to Philippa's sin. She, who loved and admired Martin, had helped his wife dishonour him.

She made up her mind firmly then to recall her cousin. She had been willing to go on with this masquerade while she thought that Philippa's holiday was an innocent one. But she would not knowingly aid and abet an illicit love affair. She thought it perfectly atrocious of Philippa to practice such deceit upon her.

Sally suddenly wept to herself.

'And I'm as bad! I'm as bad to have deceived Martin so. Oh, I wish I'd never, never started this thing.'

She felt now that she was in a labyrinth from which she would not easily escape. It had seemed simple at the start, but she must have been a fool not to foresee the appalling complications.

Even now, Sally's first thought was for Martin. What if Philippa came back from Paris in a raging temper and vented her ill feelings upon him? It would be too tragic, just as he was happy, and recovering health and strength. It was a certainty that Phil would not return in a mood to be kind or gracious. She would be furious that she had been found out and that her 'holiday' with this man, Ivor, had been cut short.

Sally, red-eyed with crying for a solid hour, walked up and down her boudoir wondering what best to do. And every time she thought of her cousin she blushed for her. It was not the frailty of human nature which shocked Sally. Neither was she the type to condemn a fellow creature. Particularly where a love affair was concerned. There was no knowing what love would do to one, or how sorely a woman in love could be tempted. But it was the way in which Philippa had gone about this thing … wheedling her, Sally, into taking her place on the grounds that she was worn out with nerves and just in need of a pleasant change – that nauseated Sally.

What worried her more than anything was the knowledge that here was Martin, believing implicitly in his 'wife's' loyalty, growing daily more certain of her affection and more hopeful about their future together. *She* had done that out of her very desire to help him. But perhaps things would only be a thousandfold times worse for him – once the real Philippa returned.

Sally worked herself up into a state of hysteria. She felt inclined to pack her suitcase and rush away and put this all behind her. Then came the customary summons from Martin. Always at this time he sent Watson for her, and they had a cigarette and cocktail together before dinner. He was able to walk to that meal now on his sticks, able to share it with her in the dining-room. The days of the couch and the trays were rapidly fading.

Sally told Watson that she would be down in a moment.

Then she gave a despairing sigh, walked into Philippa's palatial bathroom, started to sluice her face with cold water. She must not let Martin see that she had been crying. While she changed into evening dress she decided to write to Philippa to-night, tell her that she knew everything and ask her to come back. She loathed the idea of doing this. The last thing in the world she wanted was to make Martin unhappy. But she could not continue with this masquerade, deliberately encourage Phil's infidelity, and be at peace with her own conscience.

With a heavy heart, Sally put on the black velvet evening dress which Vera laid out for her to-night. She had never felt more miserable. In recalling Phil she was going to end her own happiness ... as well as Martin's. She ought never to have done this thing, so she could only expect catastrophe to be the end of it. When Vera had finished helping her dress and left her alone, Sally looked in her mirror without one single thrill although she was aware that the perfectly cut velvet dress made her look more than ordinarily slim and graceful. She wore pearls round her throat, stud pearls in her ears. Vera had brushed the fair crisp hair into great shining waves back from her forehead. Martin would appreciate this beauty. She knew that. But if she were to tell him the truth he would not find her fair. He would despise her and never want to see her again. That, she felt, was the greatest tragedy. All Martin's love and admiration were for his wife. She, Sally Browning, did not even exist for him.

Quite apart from leaving Martin, it would not be pleasant, she thought, to give up this lovely home, this luxurious bedroom which glowed with warmth from the electric radiators which had been turned on for the first time to-day. Summer was waning. The days were getting shorter, and the September heat wave had broken.

Something in Sally seemed to break to-night at the mere thought of putting Martin out of her life. She could so easily stay out her full month here. She need not make Philippa come back yet. But she *must,* now that she knew that Philippa was stabbing Martin in the back. It was as though something stronger than herself propelled her forward and she could not stop.

As she walked down the staircase to the library, she thought:

'Phil will get my letter the day after to-morrow. That means I may only have three more days with Martin.'

Three more days! There was a sick, frightened little sensation inside Sally as she contemplated that fact. Three days would pass so horribly quickly. And Martin wouldn't be happy when Phil came back. That was the worst thing of all to contemplate. *His* unhappiness. His pathetic bcwilderment when his Phil became once more the cold egotist, the selfish cheat!

Sally would have given anything to have spared Martin. But she did not see how she could prevent it. She could do nothing to put things right. The one thing she did realise was that her own punishment would begin from the hour that she walked out of this house as Sally Browning. She dared not even begin to wonder how she was going to face Rex in the future. The predominating horror was the prospect of bidding Martin a final good-bye.

Then she entered the library and found Martin seated in an armchair in front of the fire. He was wearing a dinner jacket. She had not seen him in evening dress before, and she thought how well he looked in it.

'Why, Martin!' she exclaimed, and tried to forget the bad couple of hours through which she had passed upstairs. 'You're dressed to-night!'

'Yes,' he said. 'Watson and I had a conspiracy to surprise you. Pleased?'

'Very. Are you sure it didn't tire you?'

'I'm feeling remarkably fit. All that fresh air's bucked me up. I hear it's raining now. It'll be a nuisance if we can't get out to-morrow.'

'An awful nuisance,' she agreed, 'but we can't grumble, I suppose. We've had such a marvellous summer. It's been as good as South Africa.'

'Why South Africa?'

She turned and pulled a chair up to the fire in order to hide her confusion. There were moments like these when she made little slips. How could she help it?

'Oh, I've just heard from someone out there.'

'Who?' he asked.

She hated lying to Martin, hated it so much more now that she cared for him, than she had done in the beginning. But she had no choice save to answer as the real Philippa would have done. So she stammered:

'My cousin Sally!'

And then held her breath, wondering how he would react to that name, and whether she had been mad to mention it in case it raised all kinds of possibilities in his mind. But it had no effect at all. Philippa had not mentioned her cousin Sally since they had unpacked the Browning's wedding present, and Martin did not even know that Sally had been to South Africa.

Martin was not sufficiently interested to press the point. He changed the conversation and told Sally how lovely she looked.

'Browner than ever, and so sweet!' he murmured and toasted her with his glass of sherry.

She returned the toast.

'To your continued health, Martin.'

She spoke gaily. But she was unutterably depressed.

'They're broadcasting the last act of *Othello* from Rome to-night, I see,' Martin was saying. 'Would you be very bored if we listen-in?'

She found it easy these days to control her real feelings. She just smiled and said:

'Not too bored.'

'It's a wonderful opera, Phil. And a wonderful play as old Shakespeare wrote it. I think Melchior is singing in the title-rôle. Do you remember that night when I wanted you to come with me to Covent Garden to hear him? I often wish you hadn't turned it down. I think you would have enjoyed it.'

Sally sipped her drink and thought bitterly how unlikely it would have been that *she* would ever have turned down a chance of hearing Verdi's loveliest opera. And her bitterness increased at the memory of Philippa. Oh, how crazy she must be to behave as she did and throw away those wonderful chances which Martin offered her. No doubt she preferred to go to some poker or roulette party than to attend the opera with Martin!

'I am always in sympathy with the jealous Moor,' added Martin cheerfully. 'After all, if Desdemona looked like you do, who could blame her husband for being jealous?'

Sally could find no answer for that. But she looked across at him with large tragic eyes. Poor darling Martin! What, in heaven's name, would he say if she told him this moment that his Phil was with her lover in Paris. Heaven forbid!

'Don't look at me so reproachfully, sweet,' went on Martin, still feeling happy. 'You must allow me to say nice things to you sometimes.'

'I wasn't being reproachful,' came from Sally in a low voice.

And she lowered her lashes swiftly, more afraid to-night than she had ever been of betraying herself to him.

And because of that letter which she must write to Philippa she was treasuring every moment with him ... every smile ... every compliment he paid her ... savouring the sweetness, that would be so soon dispelled, knowing that in a short while she must go away and never see him again.

'Cigarette, darling?' he said, and held out a shagreen box to her.

She took a cigarette. Her fingers were shaking. Martin noticed it. He also noticed something about her nails which he did not quite understand. They were not quite Phil's narrow pointed nails. The red lacquer was the same ... the slim brown hands were familiar ... and yet ... once or twice Martin had puzzled over her nails, and finally supposed that she was having them manicured differently, so altered their shape.

'You oughtn't to have a shaking hand, sweet,' he said. 'Very naughty of you. What is it? Too many cocktails, or late nights and nervous exhaustion?'

'You know I haven't had late nights!' Sally protested.

'I know that you've been a perfect angel to me and stayed in much too much,' he said tenderly. 'Which reminds me that I'm not going to allow you to stay in any more. This is the fourth night running that you've just sat at home and played the gramophone to me.'

'I – I went to the theatre on Monday.'

'But you usually pack a great deal more than one theatre into a day and a night, darling.'

She nodded silently. She thought:

'Phil could never, *never*, even in the earliest days, have cared about him as I do... She lives for excitement. What thrills her, bores me. I didn't even enjoy that theatre the other night because Martin wasn't there.'

'I can't be such a selfish swine as to let you make these sacrifices,' he said.

She wanted to cry out:

'But they're not sacrifices ... every hour that I spend with you is heaven to me ... if only you knew...'

But she dared not say that. She could only make some non-committal reply to the effect that 'that was all right ... that she didn't mind...'

And she seemed to remember evenings spent with Rex ... evenings when she found something missing ... when she should have been thrilled as his intended wife. Rex was always hearty and voluble. But subconsciously she had remained dissatisfied.

But now she knew why. It was because she had wanted Martin … because Martin's tender, charming personality and quick mind were the fulfilment of all her dreams. He was all that Rex had failed to be, and he alone could rouse in her the intense, almost frighteningly intense feelings that Rex had left sleeping.

Suddenly Martin was struck by some inexplicable change in his Phil to-night. There had been so many changes lately … he had almost given up trying to understand her. But he could see now that she was definitely depressed. Despite all her efforts to hide that fact, the heavy sadness which weighed her inner consciousness was manifesting itself to him.

He leaned forward and gave her a searching look.

'What is it, Phil?'

She swallowed hard and glanced away.

'What's what?' she said with an attempt at lightness.

'Something's wrong with you.'

'Nothing.'

Hard to lie to him, but she must. She must, whatever happened, keep the real truth from him.

The more that she thought about Philippa the more obvious was it that Phil, whatever she felt for this man, Ivor Lexon, did not intend to elope with him openly. Otherwise she would not have found it necessary to go away in secret. That was something ... if she meant to come back and make the best of a bad job with her husband. But would it be 'the best'? Or would her return break his heart as surely as though she had left him for ever?

Sally found no answer to any of these questions. She was lost and bewildered. She was in a maze which she had deliberately entered and there seemed no way out.

'Something *is* wrong,' persisted Martin.

He stubbed his cigarette in an ashtray and held out a hand.

'Can I help? Won't you tell me, darling?'

'No. Really, Martin, nothing's the matter.'

She had to keep a tight hold on herself. A feeling of such misery was descending upon her that she wanted to weep ... just break down and cry in his arms. She had not felt those arms around her since that moment, a fortnight ago, when he had been rather emotional with her. Lately he had not seemed disposed to be the lover in an active way. No doubt because he imagined that 'Phil' shrank from his lovemaking. But she, Sally, blindly and utterly in love, longed with all her soul to catch that outstretched hand and take what comfort he offered.

His hand had dropped and he was sitting back in his chair with a sigh.

'I suppose it's just my imagination.'

'Yes,' said Sally, and set her teeth.

'I believe you've seen too much of your husband lately. I'm sure it would do you good to have a party. Why not ask some of your friends? Where is Lexon these days? What about some dancing?'

Sally clenched her hands so tightly together that the aquamarine ring bit into her palm.

'Ivor Lexon's away. And I don't want to dance.'

That puzzled him and Sally could see it. She wished he would not discuss *her* any more. It was almost more than she could bear. She broke out:

'You're looking frightfully well this evening.'

'And feeling it. I've put on weight,' he said proudly.

'Good for you.'

'Thanks to *you*, angel. You've been such a brick lately and done so much to help.'

An expression of great wistfulness came into Sally's eyes.

'Have I really helped, Martin?'

'Why, sweet, you've been marvellous. You won't mind my saying so, will you, but you seemed to change suddenly ... to care a bit what happened to me and...'

'Oh, don't!' she broke in and caught her breath as though something in her throat choked her.

'Phil—' he began.

To her relief the butler came in and announced that dinner was served.

'Can I help you into the dining-room, sir?'

'No thanks, Denham, I can manage,' he said.

The butler bowed and returned to the dining-room.

Sally stood up and handed Martin his sticks. He rose and stood leaning upon them, and smiling down at her. So close to him she could see that his cheeks were actually filling out and that he looked younger. Younger and so terribly dear and attractive to her!

'Here goes!' he said.

As he moved forward one of the sticks slipped a little on the polished floor. Sally was quick to catch his arm. He felt a strand of the fair shining hair against his chin. The perfume of it was intoxicatingly sweet. The bare shoulder, so smooth, so brown against his was distractingly near. He lost his head, bent, kissed the shoulder, then put an arm around her and drew her near to him.

'Phil … my *darling!*…'

Sally held her breath. She knew perfectly well that this was where she should laugh and move away. But the discovery of her own tempestuous love for him was too new and too intense to be controlled easily. She knew that he wanted to kiss her. And she knew that she must let him do so … or die.

The next moment she was close in his embrace. She half supported him. The weight of him against her breast hurt and enraptured her. He covered her lips with his and she shut her eyes and was lost; answered that kiss with all her soul, with all the white hot fervour and sincerity of her love.

9

Denham stood alone in the big dining-room. The doctor and the mistress appeared to be a long time coming. He raised his brows.

'Maybe they're having a tiff,' he reflected.

Then, too well-trained to think of interfering with a second announcement, he removed the lobster soup from the side-board and sent it down to the kitchen to be kept warm.

In the library Sally faced a big crisis. For during that wild embrace, that passionate kiss, she had not been able to hide from Martin how much she loved him. And he, drunk with joy, dizzily contemplated a dream of happiness which he had long since banished, believing that it could never become reality. But to-night it was real. His Phil loved him and was his to love. Her kiss had told him so. The surrender of lips and arms had been unmistakable.

When he raised his head he was trembling so violently that Sally was alarmed.

'Martin ... you're ill ... sit down again ... let me call Watson...'

'No,' he said. 'I've never been better in my

life. It's just the sweetness of you... I'm not very strong yet ... for God's sake, don't send for Watson. Let me hold you like this ... a moment longer.'

There was nothing she wanted more. She, too, was pent up with longing. It had been such heaven, that sweet, intimate, close embrace, that it wanted superhuman control on her part, strength to deny herself a repetition of it. For the moment Rex ceased to exist in her mind. Nobody existed except Martin.

She felt his thin, sensitive fingers caress her shoulder, and press gently against the smoothness of her back. She felt distraught, like a drowning woman. But she managed to come to the surface and gasp. She said:

'No ... no ... not again ... come along... Why, Martin, how absurd we are ... dinner's waiting...'

Little gasped out sentences, squeezed out of her by the sheer necessity to do something practical before her sanity forsook her altogether. She dared not let Martin make love to her like this, *dared not*. It was bitter to watch his expression change. The light vanished from his eyes. His arms fell away from her. She knew perfectly well that once again he was telling himself that he was a fool ... that *she* had fooled him ... that he had been mistaken in thinking that her response was serious.

He recovered himself.

'Yes, I suppose we mustn't let the soup get cold,' he said.

Words wrung from him, too.

Sally's tan was deceptive, so he did not notice that her cheeks were colourless. And when she asked him if he was all right, he answered:

'Perfectly. Sorry! ... you shouldn't be so charming. I won't do it again.'

Speechlessly she turned from him and walked across the hall to the dining-room. He followed slowly on his sticks. It was still a shamble rather than a walk and he was shaking. Actually, Martin Frome was a very bewildered man. He could not for the life of him understand why his wife should have kissed him like that and surrendered so completely if she was just the old, casual Phil, indifferent these days to love-making.

Dinner was not a happy meal. Denham was quite certain that there *had* been a tiff. The doctor, who had been eating so well, seemed off his food to-night and 'her ladyship' only played with all those lovely dishes which cook sent up.

Try as she would, Sally could not regain her composure. So she said very little and Martin just made commonplace remarks for Denham's benefit. By the time they both returned to the library for coffee the atmosphere was very strained.

When Martin was seated in his winged

armchair opposite the fire, Sally smoked a cigarette and through the cloud of smoke stole a wretched glance at him. He was lighting a cigar. He looked pale and there were drops of moisture on his forehead. He seemed much more exhausted than usual to-night by the walk to and from the dining-room. His brows were knit fiercely. His whole attitude conveyed perplexity.

Sally literally agonised over him. She understood so well. He was hurt, of course ... hurt because she had refused to let him kiss her again. It was as though she had held out a glass of water to a thirsty man and then snatched it away again. It hadn't been kind. Oh, but she wanted to be kind! Her heart was breaking with the desire to make him happy. She felt that she was in the most cruel position in which any woman had ever found herself.

Without looking up at her, Martin said:

'Don't you want to go out to-night?'

'No, thanks,' she replied in a low voice.

'You can't want to sit here the whole evening. Why not ring up a friend and go and see that new Arliss film which they say is so good?'

Sally swallowed hard. She wanted to fling herself down on her knees beside him and catch his hand, put it against her cheek and whisper:

'Let me just stay like this ... with you. Oh,

Martin, I love you so!'

And instead she said:

'I really don't want to go out. I … it's raining … beastly… I think the fireside's more
comfortable.'

He cast a brief look at her. She was not
looking at him. He shrugged his shoulders
with a hopeless gesture and went on smoking his cigar in silence, brooding at the fire.
When he spoke again it was almost irritably.

'I'm quite well aware that this is all very
self-sacrificing on your part, my dear, and I
do wish you'd get out if you want to.'

Every nerve in Sally's sensitive being was
jarred. But with a hopelessness that more
than equalled his, she replied:

'Oh, no, there's no question of martyr-
dom. I assure you I'd go out if I wanted to.'

Denham entered the room.

'Major Frankham to see Mrs Frome. I've
put him in the drawing-room, madam.'

Sally stared nervously. She was thoroughly
ill at ease to-night. Who was Major Frankham? She hadn't the least idea, and couldn't
remember Philippa having even spoken of
him.

She glanced at Martin and saw that he was
regarding her with a tired, even cynical
smile. She had seen that smile before …
when she had first taken Philippa's place.
But not for such a long time. It was grim to
reflect that she had been forced to destroy

his newfound happiness.

'Frankham!' said Martin. 'So he's back! There you are, darling. An old flame to amuse you. Run along.'

Sally dared not refuse. 'An old flame,' eh? She shrank from the very thought of seeing the man, whoever he was. But perhaps it would arouse too much suspicion if she declined. Mutely, near to tears with vexation, Sally walked out of the library.

Never had the drawing-room looked more unfriendly to Sally than to-night. Handsome, stiff, formal, electric candles gleaming against the panelled walls throwing a golden glow on the polished floor. A long room and at the end of it by the famous Adams mantelpiece, a man, a stranger whom she was supposed to know intimately. He was not even down on the list of 'old friends' which Philippa had given her; people whom she was supposed to know. With a feeling of panic, she wanted to turn and rush back to the library and to Martin.

She walked across the floor. Major Frankham advanced to meet her, both hands outstretched. He was a typical Army man, precise and correct in his tails, white tie and collar, particularly white against dark sunburn. It struck her immediately that he must have just come back from abroad. Perhaps Philippa hadn't expected him and that was why she hadn't mentioned his name.

Sally took an instant dislike to Major Frankham. He had insolent blue eyes and his manner at once conveyed that he had been on very warm terms indeed with Philippa.

'Little Phil!' he exclaimed enthusiastically. 'God, but it's wonderful to see you again. Quite wonderful, my dear!'

And to her horror and consternation, Sally was seized and embraced. But she ducked her head before he could kiss her lips. After that other embrace with Martin she felt that it would have been desecration, and, in any case, something fiercely proud and reserved in Sally revolted from such intimacy with an entire stranger. She could only wonder what Philippa was made of that she could behave like this with men.

Frankham released her and stared at her hot, distressed face with complete bewilderment.

'We-ell!' was his long drawn out comment.

She crumpled a tiny chiffon handkerchief in her nervous fingers.

'How are you?' she said desperately, and wondered what his Christian name was.

'Fit as a fiddle, but might I ask how *you* are, my dear? Why the freezing reception? What have *I* done?'

'Nothing! Nothing at all!'

'Then mayn't a fellow kiss you?'

Sally's long lashes hid the distaste in her eyes.

160

'I … I didn't expect you… You see, it's *all* rather unexpected–' she stammered and broke off.

'Oh, I'm quite aware that I didn't let you know I was coming,' he said. 'But you knew that we were expected back from Gib. any day. You're the first person I've called on, I assure you, so you've no cause for complaint.'

Sally, wishing to heaven that she could be delivered from this interview, looked round her in a hunted way.

'Have a cigarette.'

'I'd rather have a drink if you'd like to offer me one.'

'What will you have?'

'Whisky and soda. But, first of all I'd like a little more warmth in the welcome.'

He seized her by the shoulders and looked down at her in a possessive way.

'Look here, Phil, you've changed. Why? What's happened while I've been away?'

Sally searched in her mind desperately for an answer. What *was* Philippa to this man? What understanding had they? How, *how* could she be carrying on an affair with this man when she was supposed to be madly in love with another … with Ivor Lexon? Were there no limits to her infidelities … to her lack of honour toward poor Martin?

'You *have* changed,' added Frankham softly. 'I can see it. And I think you owe me an explanation, don't you?'

161

'Martin has been very ill!' she said breathlessly.

'I know all about *that*. You said in your letter that he'd smashed himself up, but I don't see why that alters our affair.'

Sally felt sick.

'Well, it just does!' she broke out.

The man's insolent eyes narrowed. Then his hands fell away from her shoulders and he gave a sarcastic laugh.

'Oh? Are you telling me my day's over? I suppose I oughtn't to be surprised. You don't run anybody very long, do you?'

Sally scarlet, ashamed, remained silent. Frankham added:

'So there *is* something in the rumour about you and Lexon. While I was in Gib. I heard about it.'

'Yes, perhaps it is true,' said Sally, since there was nothing else to say.

The Major took a cigarette case from his pocket and tapped a cigarette upon it with a deliberate movement. He kept his gaze upon her.

'Well, I'm not going to be dismissed quite so crudely, my dear. You told me that day we spent together before I went out to Gib. that we'd have a good time together when I came back. And I think you owe me something, don't you? I spent the hell of a lot of cash giving you a good time. Don't force *me* to be too crude, or I'll remind you about some of

162

those horses we backed together. I rather believe I paid all the losses, didn't I?'

Sally shut her eyes. She felt in another moment she was going to be quite sick. It was going from bad to worse. So Phil had allowed this man to take her about and spend money on her; settle her racing debts. Phil, who had *Martin Frome* for her husband. It was almost more than Sally could bear. Indignation superseded caution for a moment. She blazed at the man:

'I think you're a cad. Please get out.'

'*I'm* a cad!' he echoed incredulously. 'Well, that's a fresh angle! You weren't always so particular, my dear. Let me see now ... rather a different tone in this, isn't there?'

He pulled a letter from his pocket, and she glanced at it, her heart racing. Just a few lines in her cousin's big scrawl:

'DARLING BIG PHIL, – Thanks for the sweep ticket. Missing you horribly. Come back soon. Tearing haste, but a whole lot of love.

'LITTLE PHIL.'

Sally's nostrils dilated. It was all so nauseating, so abhorrent to her nature that she could hardly endure this masquerade of Cousin Philippa one moment longer. She knew that she would *not* endure it save for the sake of that man down in the library

163

who believed in his wife.

Big Phil! The man's name was Philip, presumably. In sudden disgust Sally tore the note in pieces.

Frankham laughed.

'My dear good girl, I've dozens more.'

'Please go!' said Sally violently.

'The change of feeling has been too sudden, my dear. I can't quite believe it. And even if you're giving Lexon a run, I don't see why you want to shelve me altogether. He can dance very prettily, but I can give you a much more amusing time. What about our riding together ... that horse you asked me to get for you? Is that all going by the board?'

'Yes,' she said under her breath.

He caught her wrists and pulled her back into his arms. His attitude changed from sarcasm to passion.

'Little Phil isn't going to treat her Big Phil quite so rottenly, surely? You don't mean it, honey. You'll tell Lexon to go to the devil now I'm back, won't you?'

'No.' Sally struggled in his grasp. 'You say I've changed and I have! Let me go!'

The man stared at her, suddenly genuinely puzzled. Then he said in a slow voice:

'I may be mad, but I'd be willing to swear that you aren't the same person as the Phil I left. Not the same person at all!'

That made her blood run cold.

'W-what do you mean?' she faltered.

164

His gaze travelled over her intently.

'Just that. There's something queer about you.'

'How absurd!' She gave a short laugh. 'Isn't a woman entitled to change her mind about a man?'

'Yours is altogether too much of a change, my dear.'

Sally panted, still trying to evade his grasp.

'I may be tight,' he added. 'Probably I am. But I still can't believe you're *my* Phil.'

'Then who do you think I am?' she asked hysterically.

He let her go, his face suffusing with colour.

'Oh, I suppose you must be *you* … but it's hellishly queer to me. I've never known anybody alter so completely. You want to kick me out, do you? Well, I'm not sure I'm willing to be kicked out. You've made use of me, and I'm not the sort of fellow to stand for it. I'm going to come back, *just* when I want to. And if you treat me in this dirty way, Phil, I'll play the same tune. For instance, I don't suppose you'd like the rich and clever husband to see some of those letters you wrote to me?'

'That's blackmail!' gasped Sally.

He bowed and smiled.

'No, I'm just warning you, my dear, that I'm not the fellow to be played with fast and loose. I've been mad about you for a long time and I'm going to go on seeing you. So if you make yourself *very* inaccessible, you'll know what to expect. You can think it over. Good night.'

Sally let him go. She felt that she had not the power to call him back. With a hand to her forehead she walked out of the drawing-room, leaned over the banisters, and watched Denham show Major Frankham out.

She felt physically ill. Of all the things that had happened to her since she had taken her cousin's place, this was the worst. Of course, it was quite obvious that she could not go on. She was thankful to heaven that she had sent for Philippa. But that did not alter the situation as it was. Philippa had got herself into a hole with this man, Philip Frankham. He was not only a cad, but ready to blackmail her and use her foolish letters as a weapon to force her into his arms.

Sally pictured Martin receiving those letters. How utterly they would disgust him. There would be no end to his disillusionment if all the truth about Philippa were known.

And in another forty-eight hours she, Sally, who wanted to live and die for him, must walk out of this house and leave him alone. Alone to face the inevitable calamity of his marriage with Phil.

For a few moments, Sally stood there, her face hidden in her hands, her whole body trembling.

She must go back to Martin. But she could not face the rest of the evening with him. She would say good night and go to her room.

She pulled herself together and walked down to the library.

10

The end of another forty-eight hours marked a real crisis for Sally. To her complete surprise and consternation she received no reply to the urgent wire which she had sent Philippa.

Sally wired again. She was quite determined not to stay. Everything pointed to certain catastrophe unless the real Philippa took her place in this household again.

One of the most serious difficulties was, of course, Sally's discovery of her own passionate love for Martin Frome. She was a strong character and she could be self-controlled up to a point. But there is always a point at which even the strongest break. Sally felt she had almost reached it. She found it impossible to forget that burning and revealing moment when she had been swept into Martin's arms and returned his kiss. And now the atmosphere between them was not as friendly as it had been. Martin continued to recover health, but he seemed a little strained, a little too polite, as though he, on his part, was crushing sentiment with an iron heel.

How well she understood! Obviously he did not want to be stirred to wild emotion for 'his wife' only to be gently but firmly repulsed. And it was nothing short of torture to Sally to maintain that 'keep your distance' attitude when every instinct urged her to surrender.

Apart from her personal feelings, there was also Philip Frankham on the horizon. That detestable man with his hold over Phil and her foolish letters which he threatened to send to Martin. He did not intend to show any mercy. Within twenty-four hours of their meeting he had telephoned and asked Sally to meet him.

Sally, in order to avoid too much trouble, had tentatively arranged a lunch at the Carlton Grill. But she hoped that Philippa would be back by the time the date came. It was Philippa's mess ... and she must get out of it.

Then there was Rex. The memory of Rex hung over Sally's head like a veritable sword, waiting to pierce her. She felt so unutterably disloyal to him. She had no love left for him and no further desire to be his wife. She would rather be alone for the rest of her life than marry a man whom she did not love. Before meeting Martin she might have put up with second best, but not now ... not now, she told herself in anguish with the thought of Martin stabbing her very heart.

Long after she left Harley Street and went

out of Martin's life for ever, she would have to deal with the problem of Rex. She had made up her mind to break her engagement. But that was in the future. She was beset with immediate difficulties, and the most acute of them was her persistent longing to help Martin ... a longing which she found increasingly hard to satisfy. She felt that she was failing him. The whole thing had been a failure and the sooner it ended the better for them all.

There was no answer to the second wire to Phil. Then Sally grew really frightened. She went out to a post office and put a telephone call through to Phil's hotel in Paris. She dared not do so in the house in case any of the servants listened and suspected. But she *must* get in touch with Phil.

The wait in the post office seemed interminable and Sally's heart was heavy as lead while she hung about.

It was ten o'clock in the morning. Knowing Philippa's habit, Sally did not for a moment suppose that she would be up so early. This should be a good time to get her.

When the call finally came through, Sally stepped into the box with a slight sensation of nausea. The hand that held the receiver to her ear was shaking. The long distance line was wonderfully clear. And nothing could be clearer than the answer which Sally received, not from Phil, but from the manager of the

Crillon, who spoke perfect English. He said:
'Miss Maxwell is not here. Yes, she has *been* staying with us but she left three days ago.'

Sally's heart gave a horrid jerk.

'But has she left no address? Do you know where she's gone?'

The answer was in the negative. The manager politely assured *madam* that he did not know where Miss Maxwell had gone. He only knew that she had driven away in a car with a gentleman and had intimated that she was going down South, maybe to Nice or Cannes. He did not know. But she had said she would write later and forward an address in case there should be any letters for her.

'But are you sure?' Sally gasped incredulously. 'Are you sure she has gone South ... she hasn't gone back to England?'

The manager was certain.

Sally could do nothing more then but ask him to let Miss Maxwell have her telegrams and letters the moment she forwarded an address.

Sally was trembling as she walked out of the post office into the street. The September day was wet and grey and it was raining. Mechanically Sally hailed a taxi. A fortnight ago she would have walked through the rain, but in Philippa's lovely clothes and high heeled shoes, a taxi seemed fitting and proper.

During the drive home she was conscious of nothing but burning indignation against Philippa. It was dastardly of her to have done this. She had no right. She had promised to keep in touch with her in case anything went wrong. She must be mad. Madly in love! That was the explanation. She had driven away from Paris with 'a gentleman'. Ivor Lexon, of course. Probably she had come to the conclusion that as everything was all right at home, she might as well enjoy herself thoroughly. The longer Sally considered the matter the more desperate she became. She was caught in a veritable trap. She did not know where Philippa was. And in her casual fashion Phil might not send her address to the Crillon for days. Even weeks. Sally, her cheeks growing hotter every moment, faced the possibility that Phil might not communicate with her again until the end of the month.

'If then,' thought Sally. *'If then.'*

And her heart seemed to stop beating altogether at that thought. Phil prolonging her holiday just because she had left Sally in her shoes and knew that Sally would fill the rôle conscientiously whatever happened.

But she just couldn't go on. She couldn't stand this state of affairs for days and weeks longer. It was too much to contend with. It was a frightful strain, aping Mrs Frome, deceiving her friends, never being natural;

having to deal with people like Toni Arn-mouth and Major Frankham!

And Martin ... in heaven's name, what could she do about Martin? How could she struggle against *that* sensation interminably? No, there must be a speedy end to it all or worse calamities would follow than Cousin Phil dreamed of.

Sheer wrath against her cousin flooded Sally's being as she re-entered the Frome household that morning. Phil was behaving iniquitously. She, Sally, had just been left cold to bear the brunt of everything.

'I suppose people would say this is my righteous punishment,' Sally thought. 'I ought never, *never* to have allowed Phil to persuade me to play this crazy game.'

She went immediately to the boudoir and wrote a long indignant letter to Philippa, reproaching her for her conduct and telling her to return instantly, as she could no longer carry on.

Surely Phil would send for her mail. She would need money, yes, the need for money would drive her to get in touch with home. A hundred pounds would not last long at the rate she spent pounds, shillings and pence.

Sally now felt quite adamant on the subject of the money. She would refuse to send more. She would make Phil come back through sheer lack of funds.

But Sally did not yet know Cousin Philippa really well. There lived no woman more ruthless or stubborn when she wanted her own way.

Philippa received those letters and telegrams which were sent on to her from the Crillon.

She and Ivor Lexon were having 'a heavenly time' in a small seaside resort down South where they could spend most of the hot, sunny days in the blue water and idle away the hours in each others' arms. Neither of them had the slightest desire to return to London or the realities of their separate existence. Here they could be pagan lovers and it appealed vastly to the pagan in them both.

At first, Philippa was scared by the peremptory summons from Sally. Then, when she re-read the letters and realised that no discovery had been made, but that Sally was merely 'getting wind up' and finding the situation a little difficult, Phil shrugged her shoulders.

'I'm not going back,' she told her lover. They were sitting on the white beach under a striped umbrella, drinking cocktails following their morning swim. 'I'm going to have my whole month, if not longer. It's costing us very little to live down here and I can easily get another hundred out of Sally.'

Ivor Lexon, looking particularly handsome with a coat of deep tan on his face and graceful body, flashed his dark liquid gaze upon Philippa and said in his most melting voice:

'My beautiful! You are really happy with me, then?'

'Divinely,' she said, 'and there's nothing I'd like better than to spend the rest of my life with you, Ivor. But one must have cash, my lamb.'

After which remark Philippa took a lipstick from her bag and painted the hard vermilion curves of her selfish mouth.

'But are you sure it's safe to stay in spite of what the cousin says?'

'Absolutely. She's merely fed up because she's discovered through a phone call from that cat, Toni, that you're here with me.'

'Ah!' murmured Ivor.

'It's offending Sally's sense of propriety. But I'm afraid it must go on being offended. So long as Martin accepts her, I'm not returning. She says Martin's actually able to walk on two sticks. Who'd have thought it! That doesn't alter the situation for me, anyhow. I shall have quite enough of him when I get back.'

'Then what do you intend to do, Divine Lady?'

'Get some more money and stay where I am,' was Philippa's cool reply.

'But if Cousin Sally insists...'

175

'Cousin Sally will do as I want. I have a plan...'

And Philippa ordered two more dry Martinis and expounded the said plan to her lover.

Consequently, three days later, Sally received a letter from Philippa. And a very heart-rendering little note it was, too. There had been an accident, Philippa wrote. A most *maddening* one. Philippa had been on the very point of catching the next train home in answer to Sally's summons, when she had slipped off a rock and hurt her ankle badly. She was quite unable to walk, and the French doctor said she must not set foot to the ground before he gave her permission. That might be a week or ten days.

'So you see,' the letter ended, 'how helpless I am, Sally darling. You must hang on and help me out. It wouldn't do for there to be any discovery now. Carry on with the good work and keep Martin happy until I get home. And don't reproach me. You don't quite understand the situation, but I'll explain when I get back. Perhaps you have never known, yourself, what it is to be in love, if you did, you'd forgive me. You *must* wire me more money.'

And this time Philippa was frank and

unashamed. The money was to be wired to *Mrs* Maxwell at the Villa Rosario, Etoile-sur-Mer, near Monaco.

On the morning that Sally received this note she was not in a very good humour. She had had a difficult day with Martin yesterday. His manner had been quite abrupt, as though he resented her. He had stubbornly refused to allow her to stay with him, almost forced her to accept invitations to go out. So, instead of sitting quietly last night with the man who meant more to her now than anyone in the world, she had had to go to a boring dinner-party at Claridges, and talk to people whom she never wanted to see again, then go on to a supper at the Café-de-Paris where she had had a very unpleasant moment with Philip Frankham. He was there with another party, but had insisted upon talking to Sally. To-morrow was the date fixed for their lunch, he had reminded her, and with a sinking heart she had had to tell him that she would meet him as arranged.

She had returned home in the early hours of the morning, tired and depressed. For a moment she had stood outside the door of Martin's bedroom, a slim drooping figure in one of Philippa's gorgeous evening gowns, chinchilla cape, pale mauve orchids on her shoulders ... crushed now, with brownish stains. She had had to dance and be gay ..

177

that was what Philippa liked to do … and all the while, her thoughts had been with Martin, alone in his library. He had imagined that she enjoyed her evening. If only he had known!

Sally gave a bitter, hopeless look at the closed door and passed on to her own room.

She had slept badly, dreading the thought of to-morrow's lunch with Philip Frankham.

Then Vera brought morning tea and that letter with the French stamp.

Sally, wide awake, tore open the envelope and read what her cousin had to say. With a groan she flung herself back on her pillows. This was too much! An accident… Philippa laid up and literally *unable* to get back. That meant that she, Sally, *must* go on, for Martin's sake, if for nobody else's.

Accustomed though she was by now to Philippa's various dishonesties, it did not enter Sally's head to think this a put-up job. She took it for granted that Philippa's accident was genuine. Out of necessity, therefore, she accepted the situation. And now for yet another moment of misery! She must ask Martin for more money.

Sally put on the black suit and ivory satin blouse which Vera laid out for her. She looked unlike herself this morning, she thought. She was losing some of her tan and there were shadows under her eyes. This anxiety was beginning to tell on her. Much more of it and she would have to resort to rouge!

The maid, brushing a little face powder off Philippa's skirt, said:

'I think the weather's turned colder for good, now, madam. Will you be getting your warmer things soon?'

'I've got plenty of warm things, haven't I?' Sally asked almost irritably.

Vera looked shocked.

'But the new models for the autumn, madam...'

'I'll see about it,' Sally said shortly.

As she went out of the room Vera grimaced. 'Her ladyship' was in a tantrum this morning and more like her old self. Nobody had thought that sweet phase would last!

Sally had slept late after that late night and it was past eleven when she got downstairs. She found Martin already dressed and sitting in a chair before the library fire, signing letters which he had just dictated to his secretary.

'Good morning, Martin, how are you today?' Sally asked, trying to be bright and natural.

'Morning, darling,' was Martin's response after a brief glance at her. 'I'm fine, thanks. Feeling a bit stronger on the legs this morning.'

'That's good,' said Sally. She seated herself

179

on the arm of a chair opposite him and lit a cigarette, which she smoked thoughtfully for a moment. Of all the hateful things, asking Martin for money seemed the most hateful to her. His manner was off hand this morning, like it had been yesterday. Oh, she knew why! He was just trampling on his own feelings and of course the real Philippa wouldn't have cared how indifferently Martin behaved. Probably she would have been glad. But it hurt Sally to the quick that Martin erected this barrier and was shielding himself behind it.

He, too, lit a cigarette.

'Enjoy your party last night?' he asked.

'Very much, thanks.'

'Got a full day to-day?'

'No,' said Sally, almost angrily. 'I've a lunch engagement, otherwise I'm doing nothing. I thought you'd like to drive out to tea somewhere. It's been raining all night but the sun's struggling through now and it's not cold.'

'Thanks, dear, but don't worry,' he said. 'As a matter of fact, I think I'll go along to Bart's this afternoon. I haven't seen the inside of the hospital since my crash, and I'd like to find out how work's getting on.'

Sally lowered her lashes nervously. She felt thoroughly miserable.

'Will you be engaged the whole afternoon, then?'

'I daresay.'

She swallowed hard. So he didn't need her any more! He was just well enough now to get about and see his colleagues and think about his work and he didn't want to be nursed and amused at home! Perhaps it wouldn't matter if the real Philippa *did* come back.

And then she saw his face, that weary disillusioned face with the eyes that betrayed how much, indeed, he needed her. It was just that he was not anxious to be raised to the pinnacle of hope only to be dashed down again when he made one lover-like gesture towards her. In other words, he was treating her as he supposed that she wanted to be treated.

'You're always fixed up, aren't you?' he asked, and added lightly: 'How's Frankham? You used to be very amused by him. Are you doing any riding together?'

Sally clenched her hands.

'No,' she said in a low voice. 'I don't like him any more.'

He was making it more than usually difficult for her to ask for money, she told herself.

Martin gave her a covert look. Why the depression, he wondered. She was looking quite unhappy.

The resentment which had been his ever since that night when she had seemed to sur-

181

render – just so far as it amused her – faded away from Martin. He wanted her to be happy, at whatever cost to himself. He loved her so much. Why should she be miserable? Couldn't he give her everything that she wanted? What had happened now to upset her?

'Darling,' he said more gently, 'something's wrong this morning. I really do think you've been too kind and sweet to me lately. All the staying in and helping to make me better has bored you to tears. And now you're feeling the effects of it. Why don't you get hold of one of your woman friends and run over to Paris and buy yourself some new clothes or something?'

He was quite astonished when he saw the hot colour spring to her cheeks, and her eyes blaze at him.

'I don't want to go to Paris! And I wasn't bored sitting with you. It's not fair of you to say so … not fair!'

Sally broke off, her heart pounding, conscious that she was making a fool of herself.

Martin stared.

'Why, my dear, if you feel like that … I'm sorry. I didn't think you could enjoy being chained to my side.'

'Well, I did!'

'Why, Phil–' It was his turn to flush and impulsively he put out a hand, 'You're such a funny little thing. I don't quite understand. You change so rapidly. One moment you really lead me to suppose–' He broke off and his hand dropped. 'Oh, what's the good of trying to understand you?' he ended almost angrily.

Sally ground her teeth. It was altogether too dangerous for her to sit here and talk to Martin in this strain. In another moment she would rush across and fling herself into his arms and give the whole show away. So in despair she said:

'As a matter of fact, Martin, you do me an injustice. I don't mind at all being with you if I'm any help. But perhaps you're right when you say that I need ... a little more re-laxation ... some new clothes...' She had to force out those words, hating them, loathing herself, dreading to see the old cynical smile play about Martin's lips.

But he was gentle and understanding.

'Of course,' he nodded. 'That's exactly what I say. Well, why not run over to Paris?'

'I may later, not now. I'll do some shop-ping in town.'

'Got through that last hundred I gave you?'

Sally turned from him so that he should not see what lay in her eyes.

''Fraid I have.'

'Right. You're an extravagant child, but there it is, and I think you deserve a little spoiling. You've been spoiling me. Run

183

along and tell Swithen to make out a cheque and you can cash it and amuse yourself.'

Amuse herself! Sally felt that she would burst with misery. But she took the cheque which Miss Swithen made out and which Martin signed, and went away with it, not trusting herself to say another word to Martin otherwise she would have torn that cheque in half and burst into tears at his feet. She went straight out to the post office and wired the money to Phil at Etoile-sur-Mer, and then came back and wrote another urgent letter, begging Phil to return as soon as her injured foot would allow.

11

It was one of the most miserable days that Sally had spent since she had come to Harley Street in the rôle of Martin Frome's wife. And like a blot on the horizon was the thought of Philip Frankham, and that lunch appointment which she dared not break. With the utmost reluctance she left Martin to lunch alone and met Frankham at the Carlton Grill.

He was all that a host should be. He had ordered her a special lunch. He tried to amuse her with racy stories and chatter of horses and poker parties and scandalous anecdotes about their mutual acquaintances which was the sort of thing that amused Philippa. But it had the reverse effect upon Sally. She could not pretend to be anything but miserable during that lunch. Every now and then Frankham dropped definite little hints that he expected her to see plenty more of him and his possessive manner sickened her. Before the lunch ended he was less amiable and complaining of her chilly and indifferent manner.

'Damn it, I don't know what's the matter with you,' he groused when at three o'clock

Sally told him that she must leave. 'Why can't you spend the afternoon with me?'

'Because,' said Sally, 'I've got to take my husband out.'

That was the first excuse she could think of.

Major Frankham's eyes travelled over her in a way which made her writhe.

'My dear Phil!' he drawled, 'you'll never make me believe in this ministering angel business. It's not in your line.'

'I'm sorry, but I've told you that ... Martin's illness has made a difference.' The words came from Sally almost in despair.

'H'm, and where's the handsome Ivor Lexon?'

'He isn't in town.'

'So you really want me to think you're Frome's angel wife nowadays?'

'Oh, think what you like, but I wish you'd leave me alone.'

'I'll never do that, Phil,' he said in a low voice. 'You're too damned attractive, and the only woman who's ever held me. When am I going to see you again?'

'I'll ring you sometime.'

'I'll ring *you* up!' he said with a significant smile.

And on that note they parted. Sally went straight home and bathed and changed her clothes as though she felt that she had been in an unclean atmosphere and must wash

186

away the very memory of it.

Major Philip Frankham went to his club and pondered for some time over that lunch with the woman who had seemed hand in glove with him a few months ago. He asked himself if Philippa Frome had a double.

'I'd never in a thousand years believe that it was the same girl,' he told himself.

That conviction remained with him although he could not in anyway explain it and had no reason to believe that there was any mischief afoot.

Back at Harley Street the long day dragged itself out for Sally. She did not see Martin. But Denham told her that the doctor had been fetched by another doctor and they had gone together to the hospital.

'It's good to see how well the doctor is getting on, isn't it, madam?' the old butler murmured to Sally.

'It's fine, Denham,' Sally answered with a smile.

And went upstairs, locked herself in the boudoir so that she should not be disturbed by the maids and wept long and miserably. It was really too awful, this gnawing love for Martin which was growing, increasing day by day, in her heart. Awful and bitter to think of leaving him, leaving him to the wretched atmosphere which Philippa created in this house, to her lack of understanding and love, to her base egotism. The one thing for which

187

Sally was thankful was the knowledge that Martin's health had improved so vastly since she came. The day might even come when Martin could return to his work. Who could tell? He was walking with more assurance and his eyesight was practically normal again.

Sally heard Martin come back from the hospital. She wanted to go down to him but dared not She must go on playing her hateful part. She would have to pretend all the things that she had done; make up a tale of busy hours in the shops and fittings and cocktails, etc. The sort of things that Philippa would have done.

Leaning over the banisters, Sally just caught sight of Martin being helped to his room by Watson. No doubt he was tired after his visit to the hospital and was going to lie down until dinner.

It seemed an interminable afternoon, but at last came the time when she could change for dinner and join Martin again, without causing too much comment.

She put on the black velvet dinner dress which was one of Martin's favourites and the pearls. She thought how absurd it was that she should look forward so desperately to seeing him again, and spending a quiet evening with him, putting on records or listening to the radio. How ironic it was that hers and Phil's positions should be so entirely reversed.

Halfway down the stairs she met Watson.

'Good evening, madam,' he said. 'I was just going to tell you that the doctor isn't coming down to dinner.'

Sally stared at the little man blankly.

'Oh, but why?' she asked, feeling ludicrously disappointed.

'I think the hospital tired him, madam, so he's having his dinner in bed.'

'Is he ill?'

'Oh, no, madam, only resting. He told me to tell you not to worry about him this evening.'

Sally's nostrils dilated a little. Not to worry about him! And she had been killing time, waiting hour after hour for the moment when she could join him.

Pride came to the rescue. She forced a smile at Watson.

'Oh, very well. I've got to rush out after dinner, so it's just as well.'

Watson bade her good night, and passed on.

Sally dined alone in state, feeling so miserable that she could hardly swallow the food which Denham placed before her. Of course she had been a fool to look forward to seeing Martin. She was a fool to feel like this about him, anyhow. He did not reciprocate. He was bored with her. So bored that he didn't even want her to go up and sit with him. Well, the least she could do was to respect his point of view and leave him alone. And she did not intend to let the servants see her depression. But it was an exceedingly depressed Sally who slipped a fur coat over her evening frock and went out that evening.

She had to go out. She could not have stayed in only to sit alone. So she went to the nearest cinema and took a seat and stared blindly at the succession of pictures. She decided, there and then, that nowhere could one feel more lonely than in a place like this where everybody else seemed to have a companion, and the main topic of the films was *love … love … love…*

She stared stonily at a comedy, envying those light-hearted souls who shrieked with laughter. With scant interest she regarded the News. The 'big picture', a flaming drama, the highly artificial product of Hollywood, served only to increase her depression.

Through all the tragedy one knew that things would 'come right in the end', and the limpid-eyed heroine with her monstrous black lashes, must fall with a beatific smile into the arms of her stalwart hero and stay there. Only in life things didn't seem to come right, thought Sally … only in life!

She did not wait to see the last fervent embrace on the screen. She got up and went out and walked awhile through the damp cool streets. It had been raining while she was in the cinema. She walked doggedly, aimlessly, and wondered whether her heart would ever stop aching and longing for Martin.

At a quarter past eleven she went home. By now she was tired. Perhaps she would sleep. But she knew she was much more likely to lie awake, brooding and worrying.

She undressed, took a hot bath steaming, fragrant with scented crystals, and then slipped into the exquisite peach satin nightgown which Vera had laid out on the bed – one of those perfectly cut garments, with delicate lace across the breast and satin bows on the shoulders, which Philippa had specially made for her at a French convent.

Sally stood a moment looking at her reflection in the mirror, fingering a fold of the rich satin with the tiny frilled net hem touching her slender ankles, and thought how strange it was that nuns should make lingerie like this.

What must they think, these calm, godly women, who had dedicated their lives to Christ and to rigorous self-abnegation, while they stitched such a nightgown as this for some beautiful sensuous woman of the world to wear? Perhaps they envied the wearer. More likely they pitied her and were thankful to be shut away from temptations of the flesh.

Sally sighed a little, ran her hand through the thick bright fairness of her hair, and began to cream her face.

As she did so somebody knocked on her door.

'Who is it?' asked Sally.

Watson's respectful voice answered:

'Pardon me, madam. I was just on my way to bed, and heard the master call. I think he imagined it was you, and would like to speak to you, madam.'

Sally's heart leapt.

'Thank you, Watson. I'll go to him,' she said.

She wondered why Martin had called her. It never for an instant entered her head to refuse his request. He might be ill. So long as there was any question of his needing her, she would go to him.

With a tissue handkerchief she wiped the cream from her cheeks, dusted face and throat with powder, slipped into her chiffon velvet wrapper which tied at the back and had wide sleeves tripped with swansdown, falling almost to the hem of the gown. A bewitching enough negligée, and she looked bewitching in it.

As she walked down to Martin's room, she contemplated the fact that he had never seen her like this. She found her face and throat burning. Her whole body was tense as she knocked on his door.

'Martin, it's Phil … can I come in?'

'Hullo, yes,' came his voice.

His voice alone was enough to send the

blood rushing through Sally's veins. But she tried to appear calm and detached as she advanced to his bedside.

Martin was sitting up against the pillows, reading. A table lamp cast a dim pleasant glow over everything. This was the spare room which he had occupied since his accident, because it was on a lower floor and made less work for the servants. Green walls, green carpet, and the dark sheen of Hepplewhite walnut furniture. There were a pile of books by Martin's bedside and a tray bearing whisky and soda. The atmosphere was fragrant with the aroma of a cigar which he had smoked earlier in the evening. He looked at Sally as she entered. He had intended to be indifferent, but he knew that no man could have regarded with indifference that slim figure in the pale peach negligée. She was ravishingly fair and beautiful.

'You wanted me, Martin?' she asked.

'Why am I honoured by this visit?' he asked, without answering her question.

She stammered:

'Watson told me you called me.'

'Ah, I see! It was Watson who came past my door just now. I thought it was you.'

'Then you did call me?'

'I just meant to say good night,' he said casually.

But he told himself with bitterness that he was a fool. To-day he had decided that he had better see as little of his wife as possible. Yes, it was almost better for her to stay away and neglect him, than torment him with her presence and withhold her love.

'If I can't do anything, then I'll go,' said Sally miserably.

Martin avoided her eye.

'There's nothing you can do, thanks, my dear. Hope you had an amusing evening.'

She could have laughed.

'Oh, very amusing!'

But her eyes were resentful as she gazed at him. He looked young and attractive in that pyjama suit which was of thick creamy silk, buttoned high at the neck, Russian-wise. His dark, crisp hair was ruffled like a boy's and the glow from the lamp gave him colour.

'I enjoyed seeing the hospital again,' suddenly he remarked.

Sally toyed with the swansdown on her sleeve.

'I'm sure you enjoyed it, Martin.'

'There was a time when I honestly thought I'd never see that operating theatre again.'

'Well, you don't feel like that now. You know you're going to get much better and be able to go back to your work.'

Martin drew a deep breath.

'So they all tell me.'

'And you'll like that?'

'Lord, yes!' he said, enthusiastically, then

added: 'Stenning was saying this morning that he thinks I ought to get away for a change.'

Sally looked at him quickly.

'Yes?'

He avoided her gaze.

'He suggested that I should go abroad, but I don't think I want to particularly. I might run down to Devonshire.'

'When?'

'Oh, any day now. Nothing to stop me getting into the car and being driven down there.'

Sally's heart began to beat really quickly. Did that mean Martin was going to ask *her* to go away with him? That would complicate matters considerably ... and with Philippa not even on the way back...

Martin thought he detected uneasiness on her face. He mistook the meaning and said quickly:

'My dear, why the gloom? I won't drag you with me, I promise you. You've been bored quite enough.'

Sally's already torn nerves seemed to snap. She jumped to her feet, her cheeks scarlet.

'Why do you keep saying that I've been bored? I haven't ... I *haven't!*' she said furiously.

And almost as soon as she had spoken she knew that she'd been mad. But she could not bear him to treat her with this indifference, or let him go on feeling that he was not wanted, and it was only when she needed more money that she was sweet to him. Yes, that was what he must think, and it was beyond her endurance.

Martin ran his fingers through his hair with a bewildered gesture. He stared at Sally's flushed, furious little face.

'My dear Phil, what is it? Have I said the wrong thing again?'

She did not answer. No words came. She was on the point of bursting into tears. He could see her breast rising and falling. It was obvious that she was upset, very upset, and he was completely at a loss to understand her.

'Darling,' he said, 'I suppose you don't by any chance *want* to come with me?'

Still dumb, she looked at him. But the expression in her eyes was more eloquent that words. It gave her away hopelessly. No man on earth could have mistaken it, betraying as it did all her passionate longing and adoration.

And Martin Frome met that gaze fully and was staggered by it. The next moment he put out both hands and pulled her down on to the bed.

'Phil … Phil, what do you want me to think … when you look at me like that? Good God, child, I'm not made of stone. I'm only flesh and blood and it's not fair of you to try me too far. Anybody'd think you were unhappy because I wouldn't go out with you this afternoon. But that's ridiculous. Until lately you've never had five minutes to spare for me. But your eyes... Phil, tell me the truth, what do you feel about me? What do you want *me* to feel about *you?*'

She lay across him, breathless, half delirious with the ecstasy of being in his arms again. Caution was flung to the winds. She forgot everything except that she loved him and that he wanted her love.

His fingers were stroking her hair, her shoulders, the lovely curve of her body under the satin wrapper. He pulled her nearer him and whispered:

'Don't you realise that I'd give my whole life to know that you loved me a little this way?'

And then Sally, with her lips against his ear, answered:

'I do ... I do.'

He drew a deep breath.

'Then if that's so, nothing on heaven or earth can hurt me any more,' he answered.

For one wild moment she was tempted to tell him everything. It would have been so wonderful that she was not deceiving him, that she was just Sally, and to be loved by him as Sally. But she dared not speak.

He was whispering:

'Oh, darling, I seem to have waited the

longest years of my life for this one hour.'

She put her cheek, wet with tears, against his.

'I love you!'

'It's like a dream. Tell me I'm not going to wake up, my sweet … tell me…'

She clung closer and answered:

'No, no. It isn't a dream. It's true.'

She felt his lips upon her mouth. Lips that clung and burned, long wild kisses that succeeded each other until her whole body seemed on fire with love for him. She knew that she was lost and mad. But she had told him that she loved him and she was going to prove it whatever calamity ensued.

The grey September dawn filtered through a chink in the green and gold curtains of Martin's room, and found him staring intently at the lovely face in the crook of his arm. Lovely with the shadows of sweeping lashes on cheeks still pale golden from the kiss of the sun, and red lips still warm from the kisses of a lover.

But Martin's eyes were darkly stern and his brain was a chaos of doubt, filled with a staggering astonishment.

His lips formed a voiceless query to the slumbering woman.

'If you are not Philippa, my wife, *then in God's name, who are you?*'

12

For the first time in his life, Martin Frome played detective in his wife's room; a thing which under normal circumstances he would never have dreamed of doing. But these were circumstances anything but normal. Indeed, Martin found himself so stupefied that it was only with the greatest difficulty that he managed to get through that morning without giving himself away. Time and time again he was on the verge of telling this girl that he *knew* ... demanding an explanation. But something held him back. Perhaps the desire to say nothing until he, himself, had found out a little more. And, of course, there was in the back of his mind the utter dread of knowing the truth; of seeing this lovely bubble of illusion burst before his sight and vanish for ever.

Whoever she was, he loved this girl who called herself his wife and who had climbed the dizzying heights to the very stars with him last night. Loved or hated her, which? This morning he scarcely knew. He was only conscious of the fact that he was the victim of an unspeakable and incredible deception. He wanted to plumb it to the depths before he said a word.

He pretended to be sleeping when Sally went to her own room. But he was wide awake and rang early for Watson to help him bath and dress.

Watson, as he laid out the doctor's clothes for the day, sniffed the air suspiciously, filling his nostrils with the delicate perfume of *'Vol-de-Nuit'*, not that he could have given it a name. But it gave him something interesting to report to the staff. So far as he could see, the doctor and 'her ladyship' appeared to be having a second honeymoon.

Martin waited until he heard Philippa's bathroom door shut. Then slowly and carefully, with the aid of his sticks, he went upstairs into his wife's bedroom.

It seemed a long time since he had entered this familiar, luxurious nest. It looked inviting enough with the electric fire gleaming, throwing up the sheen of the rich peach-taffeta draperies, all the glittering array of bottles on the circular dressing-table, and roses by the bed. Late summer roses which he had sent her yesterday.

Martin's heart seemed to pound until it hurt him. The perfume of this room was so redolent of *her* ... and the very warmth and beauty of it recalled her loveliness, her bewitching surrender, and the breathless dream which had ended in all the amazement of his discovery.

But he must move quickly, before Phil emerged from the bath. Of course he would have an excuse ready if she found him here. But he would rather she did not come at the moment. To pry into another person's belongings was so foreign to him that he almost hesitated before he acted. Then, feeling himself justified, he went ahead.

It struck him that the best place to look for evidence of what he wanted would be in that green Russian leather bag with the silver clasp, lying on the dressing-table. *Her* bag. Breathing quickly, Martin opened it and went through the contents. He found two letters. One with a South African stamp. One in a handwriting which seemed vaguely familiar and which bore a French post-mark. He opened the latter.

The very first words caused him an electric shock. They also gave away the truth at once.

'*My dear Sally.*'

Sally … of course, what a fool he'd been! Sally Browning, Philippa's cousin who was supposed to be as like her as though they were twins. He had never seen her but Phil had told him about the cousin whom she had played with as a child. They had often been mistaken for each other, she had told him. That, then, was the explanation of the amazing resemblance between the two women. It was *Sally,* who, last night, had lain in his arms and whom he had loved as he had never loved Philippa and perhaps would never love again.

He read the letter through to the end. The whole truth crowded upon him. It was more than an ordinary shock.

Twice he read what was written in that letter which came from *his wife* … twice to the bitter end he absorbed every word until the facts were clear. Then with his brain reeling and the sensation that he was in some fantastic dream, he walked slowly on his sticks out of the lovely bedroom and down the stairs, one by one, into his own room. Watson was there, putting away clothes. Martin did not want to face Watson, nor anybody, for a while. He wanted to be alone. He trembled violently and his brow was pouring with perspiration. He felt physically ill. But somehow he managed to go down yet another flight and reached the library. Once there he closed the door and sank heavily into his armchair. Throwing the sticks on the floor he buried his face in his hands.

It was some time before he began to analyse the situation. Bit by bit he pieced the facts together and unravelled the mystery. He faced the crude and unlovely truth. First that Philippa no longer cared whether he lived or died, and had a lover … Ivor Lexon … and had gone away with him to the South of France. Secondly, that this girl who had been living with him for the past few weeks was Phil's cousin, Sally Browning.

Why had Sally done this thing? That was not quite so clear to him as other points in the case. But there could be only one reason. Money!... Phil had paid her. She was 'a poor relation' and probably needed cash. That did not excuse her in Martin's sight. It seemed to him unforgivable that any girl should consent to aid and abet such a deception. Sally must be thoroughly bad to have consented to it.

The longer he considered the affair the more angry Martin grew. He felt violently incensed against this girl. Monstrous of her to condone his wife's infidelities and consent to this masquerade! An excellent plan from Phil's point of view, of course. She had no desire to be divorced and disgraced. This must have seemed a splendid idea; an easy way of eating her cake and having it, and Sally could not have one scrap of conscience.

There seemed no room in Martin Frome's mind at this crucial hour for disappointment in Philippa. The thing was too big and shattering to allow for common, petty grievances. Neither did it seem to matter so much that Phil was faithless, the instigator of this cunning intrigue. It was the girl upstairs who mattered. This Sally who for the last fortnight had beguiled her way into his heart so completely and absolutely.

All his emotions were concerning Sally, most of his anger was directed against her.

Phil seemed remote, detached from him, something outside the immediate circle of his feelings. But he dwelt on the thought of Sally until her image and everything she had said or done seemed to dance in letters of fire before him.

He understood so many things now. One by one he recalled little incidents which had baffled him. The subtle differences between Phil and Sally. He must have been crazy ever to be misled in the first place. God, but it was laughable that a man shouldn't know his own wife. The explanation, of course, was that he had been a very sick man when the two girls had first changed places. He was lying in a darkened room, and he had not been on very intimate terms with Phil. Easy enough at the start!

Then, of course, there had never been any reason why he should doubt that she was Phil. Why should he have suspected intrigue? There had been nothing so far as he knew to promote suspicion. Never in his wildest dreams had he suspected such a thing as this. It was unreal – a good story for a film, he told himself. Yet if one saw it on a film or read it in a book it might hardly be credited.

And Phil had done this to him!

Sally had done it. Shaking from head to foot Martin raised his head and looked up at the

204

ceiling as though his eyes would pierce the two floors and reach that bedroom in which Sally was now dressing. She, who so closely resembled Phil that even *he* had not guessed; she whose voice, whose walk, whose colouring were Phil's, in every detail.

Truly, the physical resemblance was an astonishing one. But now it struck him that the personalities of the two women were different. There had been none of Phil's hardness or coldness in Sally. She had been soft and kind and sweet. He almost laughed aloud as he recalled the past few weeks. He had been so surprised at 'Phil's' change of attitude. Little wonder. It was Sally Browning who had devoted her time to him. And why? Not because she was really anxious to be kind, but because of what she could get out of this business.

Martin took a handkerchief from his pocket and wiped his forehead. He felt weak, and sick. He was incapable of moving and could only sit there, turning the thing over and over in his mind.

It struck him that the cruellest part of this cruel masquerade had been Sally's line of conduct. It wouldn't have mattered so much had she continued to be the cold, inaccessible, difficult Philippa. But she had seemed to care for him and had brought him utterly to her feet.

Then the climax of last night…

Never while he lived would Martin understand last night. For he would have sworn on any oath that that girl in his arms loved him. She had told him so again and again during the wild sweetness of their hours together. Long after he had begun to doubt ... long after he had realised that she was not Phil ... he had wondered why she should take the trouble to mislead him so with her passionate surrender. And he could only take it for granted that there was a generous streak in her which had made her feel that somehow she must pay her debts. She had got money, clothes, a good time out of the whole business, so she had felt it her duty to give him love, or the semblance of love in return.

Her duty! Martin shivered uncontrollably and let his head drop back into his hands. That was what hurt. That was the most bitter thought of all. Last night Sally had acted just as she had done during the rest of the time. A very clever, consummate actress she was, too. Whilst he, poor fool, had been deliriously happy believing that he had won his wife at last.

That was the unforgivable sin she had committed. The masquerade of loving! And she would find that it did not put paid to the bill. For the first time in his whole life Martin Frome was conscious of the desire to hurt someone as he had been hurt.

He could think of a dozen different ways of treating this business. The most simple and direct method, of course, was to turn Sally out of the house, first telling her what he thought of her, then file a petition against his wife.

But that seemed too simple. He did not see why Sally should get away with the game as easily as all that. No! He made up his mind then and there to say nothing at all for the moment. Sally could carry on with her game and he would watch and wait. He would be coldly amused to see what next she would do, and what line Philippa would take with him when she returned.

If he had been a psycho analyst instead of a surgeon, what a store of treasure he could draw upon, he thought ironically. Surely this must be a unique affair!

The more he thought about it the more coldly and quietly angry he became. They had tricked him, these two ... his wife and her cousin ... they had been without mercy. They had built up nothing but misery for him. Between them they had annihilated his most cherished dreams. While his body had been recovering they had seen to it that they destroyed his soul.

And still he could not think of Philippa or care about her ... she could go to the devil, she and her lover! He had poured out his devotion upon her for years and received nothing in return! It was Sally, Sally, SALLY, upon whom he concentrated ... and whose memory tortured him. He loved her. He loved all the sweetness and gentleness and the bewitching beauty of her. God, but he could go upstairs and kill her now for making him love her like this! She should not get off too lightly. He would see to that.

He must try to give her her due. She had been his inspiration these last few weeks. Possibly he had her to thank for his wonderful progress. And there his debt to her ended. He would never forgive her for last night, because he could never *forget*. Therein lay the sting.

Denham knocked on the door and announced that breakfast was waiting in the dining-room.

'Right,' said Martin. 'I'll be there.'

But he could not rise from his chair. He felt as though his legs were weighted. This shock had not done him much good, he thought. It had set him back a bit. But what did he care? What did he care about anything anymore? He only knew that in the near future, Sally Browning would make her exit from this house and out of his life as suddenly and dramatically as she had made her entry. Then he would be faced with Philippa. Of course, he would not go on living with Philippa after what he knew. That was impossible. So ended his hopes of peace, of happiness in the future.

He wondered what in the name of heaven his medical colleagues, his many friends would say if he opened their eyes to what had been revealed to him this morning.

It all seemed so contemptible. And so far as Phil and her cousin were concerned there was little to choose between them. They were as culpable as each other. He might have forgiven Phil if she had really loved Ivor Lexon and been frank and honest about it. But she had been cowardly – too cowardly even to make an elopement. He loathed moral cowardice. As for Sally, she was mercenary. He loathed that, too. And Phil was mercenary. Sally was sending money to her. Between them they were bleeding him.

Then he remembered a paragraph in the letter which he had just read. From that it might be inferred that Sally had not known that Phil had gone away with a lover. Martin was baffled by that for a few moments. But he gave up trying to understand the thing in detail. He could only see it as a whole, and there seemed little or no excuse for anything Sally had done.

The library door opened. Martin looked up. Sally came in, Sally looking fresh, radiant, more beautiful than he had ever seen her, her eyes star-bright in the warm carnation bloom of her face, her fair hair glistening, waving crisply back from her smooth forehead. Sally in a tailored suit which showed so plainly the perfect lines of her figure, and a silk plaid blouse with a little bow at the throat which made her look ridiculously young.

The smile which she gave Martin was sweet and shy. At least he might have thought that it was shy if he hadn't known the truth about her now. But how could any woman capable of such deceit be as sensitive and reticent as Sally would like him to believe?

'But how early you are!' she said. 'I didn't think you'd be up.'

He tried to speak. He tried to smile, but felt that his features must have twisted into a humourless grimace. He had undergone an hour of such mental strain that he was physically affected. Mutely he put a hand over his eyes.

The radiance was extinguished in Sally's limpid eyes. With an exclamation she rushed forward and knelt beside him.

'Martin! What is it? Oh, my darling, are you ill?'

He almost shrank visibly as he felt her weight against his arm and her hand touch his hair. Bitter and sweet, too agonisingly sweet, the touch, the scent of Sally and the intoxicating reminder of last night. He had adored her. In this moment he felt savage, far removed from a quiet, composed medical man whose name was famous in Harley

Street. There was a primeval instinct urging him to put his fingers around her soft brown throat and squeeze the life out of her and tell her that she had murdered his soul.

Sally looked at him in horror. She could see that he was bathed in perspiration, and feel his trembling. Curiously enough it did not enter her head that he had discovered the truth about her. He had accepted her for so long and last night had become lover as well as husband, and there seemed no reason to believe that things were any different this morning. She took it for granted that he was ill.

'Martin, my dearest, you shouldn't have got up ... you should have stayed in bed and rested. You had a long tiring day at the hospital, and...'

She said no more but flushed gloriously, and Martin, unshielding his eyes, looked at her, saw that tender, sensitive colour and gritted his teeth. Why in God's name should she blush? Why act? Why behave as though she had truly loved him and with all her heart was concerned for him. He wanted to push her away. He wanted to drag her in his arms and kiss her brutally. He remained silent, his mouth dry, his face livid.

'Martin!' cried Sally in a stricken voice. 'Oh, I had better call Watson ... send for Dr Stenning...'

And then at last he spoke. He knew if he

did not say something, do something, it would strike her in a moment that her secret had been revealed to him. And he was not going to let her know yet. No. Not yet!

'Wait,' he panted. 'Don't call Watson. I'll be all right in a moment.'

'You're ill. Is it your heart? Oh, Martin, you're not as strong as you thought...'

He could have laughed. Nothing was wrong with his heart. And he was stronger than he had been since his accident. Last night with the warmth and passion of her lips against his, and his fingers threading through the ash-gold of her hair, he had been a super-man, a god, a mortal who had been raised to Olympian heights and tasted ambrosia from the hands of Venus, of Psyche, of the loveliest of the immortal goddesses who had taken shape in the divine form of his wife.

Wife! ... no, it was this girl who knelt beside him with her lovely anxious eyes and slim brown hands ready to caress, and who was a living lie, she was enjoying her masquerade. Wanton as well as heartless maybe. How did he know? What did he care? If only he had died last night ... before he knew...

And then he seemed to grow very cold and calm. He remembered a lecture which he had heard when he was a medical student ... one of the senior men at the hospital had discussed hysteria. It was more prevalent amongst women than men, he had said, but in moments of great stress even the strongest man might find himself in the grip of it. And this was the one moment in Martin Frome's life when hysteria threatened him, and he did not know whether he wanted to laugh or weep or do both, hideously.

But he conquered it as he had conquered everything else in life. There was an indomitable streak in him, and he was not prepared to throw away his manhood because of a girl's heartless duplicity.

He said quietly:

'I'm better now. Perhaps it *was* my heart ... just a little attack ... maybe I came down the stairs too fast ... anyhow I'm all right now.'

'Thank God!' said Sally.

He looked at her with penetrating eyes. She seemed relieved. Perhaps she was. Perhaps she was one of these inconsequent people with no genuine feelings, yet with a certain amount of sympathy and surface kindness. She was deceiving him, wrecking him, but she wanted to do it nicely. He grew sarcastic and would like to have shown it. But before he could speak again, Sally had bowed her head on his knee and was saying:

'Martin ... Martin, what would I do if anything went wrong with you!'

He looked down at the bent pretty head. The pale autumn sunlight drifting into the sombre library made a silver halo of that head. He could feel the warmth of her cheek against his knee. Warm and pink like a sun-kissed peach and was velvet soft for lips to touch. Much too lovely and desirable. He clenched his hands as though afraid to touch her. But he had to take out a hand-kerchief and wipe the moisture from his forehead.

Now he could see what a fool he had been! Now he could tell the difference between Phil and Sally. So easy to tell once he *knew*. Phil, even in the early days of their honey-moon, had never been quite like this; had never been one to sit at his feet and adore. She had always wanted to be the adored, the passive recipient of his caresses. However much he resented Sally Browning's part in this game he could never deny her generosity.

Anger gave way to grief ... an immense and crushing grief because he had grown to love an image, an illusory person who had flashed into being and then faded. And he wanted to go no loving and believing, wanted to with all his heart.

He was a fool to be soft about it, he told himself grimly. This ought to have made a hardened cynic of him. But he had suffered greatly since his accident and had many battles to wage. He was tired of pain and it had seemed so grand and glorious to enter that paradise of delusion yesterday. Yesterday might be a thousand years ago. To-day it was as though life was a blank and nothing could ever make him happy again. Nothing but his work. That must be his objective now ... to get well and to go back to his work and put women out of his life.

He tried to think about Philippa, to dwell upon her dastardly behaviour. How could she have repaid his devotion and fidelity in this way? It was incredible. And yet he could feel no jealousy. Yesterday, before he knew the truth, he would have been jealous. It would have broken his heart to think that behind his back, his wife was stealing an illicit honeymoon with another man. To-day it didn't seem to matter so much what Philippa had done. And that was because all his feelings had become concentrated upon this girl who knelt on the floor beside him with her head against his knee. He could not divide his feelings. For him, Philippa, his wife, and Sally were still one. It was going to take him a long time to dissociate them; to remember that they were two ... and that the one who really belonged to him was not here, had never loved him and never would love him in this life.

Sally raised her face. Her eyes, more grey than blue, under the sweeping fringe of lashes, smiled at him mistily.

'Are you sure you're all right now?'

He nodded.

'Yes.'

'Shall we have some breakfast? Or would you like me to bring yours here?'

Again he nodded.

'I do feel a little weak. Get Denham to bring me in a tray. Only coffee.'

'Nothing to eat?'

'No.'

'Oh, Martin!' cried Sally in distress.

He felt almost inclined then to say something brutal, to tell her that she was a little liar and schemer and that she didn't really care whether he ate or didn't eat.

The expression on his face baffled Sally. Why was he being so curt, almost cross with her? Why hadn't he touched or kissed her?

And then the hot blood surged in crimson waves across her face and throat again. Slowly she rose from her knees and stood with downcast eyes, pulling at the little bow on her blouse. It struck her in sudden dismay that Martin was different this morning because ... of last night. Perhaps men were like that. The morning-after meant 'sad satiety'. This morning Martin was a little bored. But that was surely not his character. She could imagine Rex behaving like that. But not Martin. He was so charming, so sensitive a lover.

Phil, of course, would think she had been a fool. Phil wasn't generous. Perhaps it didn't pay to be generous. Sally was thoroughly baffled and unhappy. And Martin realised the fact and thought:

'I suppose I must make an effort to be a little more agreeable or she'll find out that I know.'

He held out a hand.

'All right?' he asked.

Almost immediately she was back and beside his chair and somehow or other she was in his arms and she was whispering:

'Martin, darling ... *darling...*'

He held her in almost a despairing clasp. He pressed her face against his shoulder and looked over her head at nothing. But he cried within him:

'Why have you done this? Why, *why* did you allow ... last night? It wasn't kind. It was monstrous!'

Sally in his arms was happy again. There was something almost pagan in the quality of her new-born love for Martin. She more than loved. She worshipped him. And the great and intense feeling for him swept everything else out of her mind. Nothing else seemed to matter except the wish to love him and to go on being loved by him. She drove from her thoughts the knowledge that the end was in sight and that only too soon Philippa would come back and that she must give up this marvellous and shattering love which had come into her life. She tried not to think at all; merely to go on blindly, believing that Martin, in his ignorance, was as happy as she was; never for an instant guessing that *he knew*.

13

Sally sat staring at a pile of unpaid bills on the French painted desk in her boudoir. In helpless fashion she examined them. Huge bills from the most fashionable costumiers and modistes in London and Paris; from Molyneux, Worth, Chanel; from Pinet where all Philippa's shoes were made; from Antoine where her hair was coiffeured, from big stores where she ran up a dozen and one accounts for dozens of little things.

Nearly all of them had that polite but somewhat final request for payment. Philippa, the wildly extravagant, had let them all wait. What she had done with her allowance, Sally could not think. She had just frittered it away; probably at poker parties and race meetings.

One thing Sally did know, and that was that she could not attempt to pay any of them and did not intend to ask Martin for another penny. Philippa must come home and settle her own debts. After last night it was more than Sally could bear to demand a shilling from *him*.

She put the bills away in an Italian leather blotter, lit a cigarette and sat smoking, knees hunched up, arms folded round them. There was a queer, almost frightened look in her large eyes.

When she had gone to her own room early this morning to bath and dress she had felt that she was living in some strange and lovely dream. She had been in an exalted state of mind and body, tremendously excited and happy, conscious of an utter fulfilment and content. She loved Martin madly, yes, madly was the word. Everything about it was mad … everything that she had done. And yet she could not stop loving him and could not regret one single hour of that ecstatic night.

But now it was as though she had suddenly walked through a gate which shut out ecstasy and brought her to a roadway of grim reality. Some of the madness had passed. She was awaking from delirium and becoming conscious of facts again. And she realised what she had done.

She had realised it when, this morning, she had first faced Martin in the library. He had seemed peculiar and ill-at-ease with her. True, she had ended in his arms, but only for a few moments. Then he had seemed reluctant to carry on the rôle of lover and had suggested breakfast in a mundane fashion. After that he had told her that he must do some work. He had been in the library with Miss Swithen writing letters ever since.

Sally felt shut out ... shut out of that room and outside the circle of his love. She told herself that she had had no right ever to enter it. She had been more than mad. She had been utterly wrong.

How could one see things in their real perspective in such fevered hours as those spent in Martin's arms? Impossible! But apart from him she could and must see straight, she told herself. She ought never to have surrendered in that insensate fashion. She should have controlled her feelings. At the time, she had excused herself on the grounds that she was making *him* happy. But now it no longer seemed sufficient excuse. That she had done irreparable harm to herself and been flagrantly disloyal to Rex did not seem so bad as the fact that she had hurt Martin. She had given much ... yet she had hurt him. When Phil came back, her ordinary cold, ungenerous self, Martin would be made doubly conscious of his loss. And of course she imagined that he would never understand, merely be baffled and perplexed and unhappy about it all.

Sally extinguished her cigarette, and then drew the back of her hand across her eyes. Every beat of her heart seemed an ache this morning. It was almost more than she could do to contemplate the terrible unhappiness ahead of her when she must leave Martin for ever. She only knew that she *must not* allow any repetition of last night. It was unfair to them all.

She pulled herself together and started to write a letter to Rex. She must break her engagement now and at once. It might hurt Rex for a while but not so much as she would hurt him by marrying him without love. It was quite impossible even to contemplate a union with him now. After this she would never marry, she told herself. She would rather just work and be alone and dedicate her thoughts, herself, to the memory of Martin.

Half-way through the letter she read what she had written. She tore it up. It seemed so awful to be sitting here writing to Rex saying: *'I can't go on with our engagement…'* She had given him her word. She had said good-bye to him when she had left South Africa as though she loved him. He was relying on her. She felt so mean … and yet … she had never really loved him. And surely it would be meaner still not to give him a square, honest deal?

She did not get very far with the second letter. Her thoughts were confused and her fingers shook so that she could scarcely hold the pen. She was not really in a fit state to write to Rex this morning. She was too nervous, too strung up.

Finally she put on a hat and went out. The September day was chilly and misty. She

222

was glad of the rich softness and warmth of the summer-ermine coat which Vera had handed her; a short coat with a little fur tie which looked very smart with her tailored skirt. Yet somehow this morning she hated Philippa's luxurious clothes; hated Philippa herself. She wanted nothing that was Philippa's ... save Martin. And he was the one possession for which Phil had little use.

Sally took a taxi to the Bayswater boarding-house where she had been staying when she first returned from abroad. Her heart sank at the sight of the gaunt depressing house, the bay windows with the Nottingham lace curtains, and the thought of that unsavoury odour of cooking which she knew would assail her nostrils as soon as she went into the front hall. She would be going back to all this soon. She would cease to be Mrs Martin Frome and would become Sally Browning again. Complete and utter separation from Martin. Only that mattered ... only that.

No sooner was Sally in the house than Miss Potting, the proprietress, emerged from the back of the hall and hailed her.

'Why, Miss Browning, I've been wondering when you were going to call for your mail,' she said, gasping. She was always in a state of heavy breathing and panting. She was a stout woman and had a great many stairs to climb in the service of her 'guests' as she called them. She eyed Sally's slim, exquisitely dressed figure with faint disapproval. There was some mystery about the young woman from South Africa, and no mistake. It seemed queer that she should have gone off at a moment's notice like she did at the beginning of the month, leaving all her luggage here, and just turning up from time to time to collect letters. Look at that coat she was wearing too! Miss Potting was a virtuous spinster and had spent her life among others like herself. And she was a little afraid whenever she saw a young woman in an expensive fur coat that it was a badge of shame. Miss Browning was a nice girl and had been thought well of when she had first arrived from South Africa. But now Miss Potting was not at all sure that she was 'nice'.

A little frigidly she said:

'A boy came yesterday with a cablegram for you. I told him I'd keep it and deliver it when you turned up.'

Sally felt herself going hot.

A cablegram! That could only be from Rex. She said:

'May I have it, please?'

Miss Potting brought the orange envelope and a letter. Sally stood in the dark little hall gazing at them. The letter was from Rex's mother. She tore open the cablegram and read it. It said:

'Great news stop expect me Tilbury October 1st Angerry Castle stop Rex.'

Sally felt physically sick for a few moments. Her throat seemed to dry up. That radio-gram had been sent from the boat. The *Angerry Castle* must be at Malta now. And in a week's time Rex would land at Tilbury. But why? And what was the great news? She was staggered. The last thing she had anticipated was the sudden arrival of Rex in this country. And it was the last thing on earth that she wanted. It would complicate matters horribly. Particularly if Phil was not back. What in heaven's name would she do? Rex might arrive here and ask for her, and then find that she was at Harley Street.

Sally felt this to be the final catastrophe. And it only proved to her for the hundredth time that she had been mad ever to consent to such a masquerade.

She stuck the cablegram in her bag and opened Mrs Trencham's letter. The very sight of the thin spidery writing on violet notepaper brought a somewhat painful vision of Rex's mother. She was rather like her writing, thin and spidery and domineer-ing. A shrew who had her husband well under her thumb and who spoiled her son upon whom she lavished all her devotion. Sally had not taken very kindly to her future mother-in-law and it was quite certain that Mrs Trencham was jealous of her. But she had liked Rex's father; a harmless, genial old man bullied by his wife and treated with faint contempt by Rex.

Mrs Trencham's letter explained everything.

It was not very affectionate and had obviously been written because her son had insisted. It presented Sally with 'the great news' in no very glowing terms. It just told her that Mrs Trencham was writing because Rex was too rushed and excited and busy to do so himself, and to warn her of their arrival in England. *Their arrival.* That meant both Rex and his mother. The old man had been left in Johannesburg. Rex had come into money. A lot of money. Mrs Trencham's brother, a South African diamond merchant, who had made most of his pile before the war and kept it, had just died without issue leaving Rex everything. Rex had not even known that he was his uncle's heir. In fact, the said uncle, who was a great traveller, had not really communicated with his sister for the past ten years. But he had returned to Johannesburg, his birthplace, there to die, and Rex and his mother had gone to see him in his last moments. Then Rex woke up one morning to find himself a rich man.

'Of course,' Mrs Trencham's letter ended, 'we can take it for granted that Rex will wish for an immediate marriage in London, and then we propose to return to South Africa.'

Sally walked blindly out of the boarding-house, stepped into a taxi and was driven back to Harley Street. Her thoughts were in such chaos that she could hardly collect them. She walked into Philippa's boudoir and unlocked a drawer, and took out the half finished letter to Rex. Standing there in coat and hat, she stared at what she had written; the difficult words telling Rex that she had found out that their engagement was a mistake and that she wished to break it. In a despairing way she tore the letter in little bits and flung them into the waste-paper basket. Too late! Three weeks too late. Rex and his mother were on their way here. The boat was due in on October 1st. That was a week from to-day.

Fast and hard beat Sally's heart. Her face was white under the fading coat of tan. Her eyes looked enormous, and afraid. She was in a terrible quandary; she felt almost that she was in a trap. And in a measure she had fashioned that trap for herself. Well, she was beautifully caught. Here she was, masquerading as Mrs Martin Frome, madly in love with Martin, fully determined to break with Rex. And Rex, now a rich man, was descending upon her, demanding immediate marriage.

Her fingers flew up to her cheeks. She gave a little shudder.

'No,' she said aloud. *'No!* I couldn't *now.'*

One thing stood out clearly in her mind. She must get away from here and become Sally Browning again before she faced Rex. Of course, she would *have* to see him and tell him that she could not marry him in spite of the money. A hateful thing to do, when a man had rushed across the ocean to claim his wife! But she had no alternative after yesterday.

The only thing she must do was to prevent a scandal; prevent an unpleasant meeting, for instance, between Martin and Rex. That would be too frightful! She knew Rex and his blustering temper only too well. A temper not easily provoked, because he was good-natured, but like his mother, if he felt himself injured, he would not hesitate to be vindictive.

Whatever occurred he must never find out that she had spent these weeks in Philippa Frome's place.

Then fresh anxiety assailed Sally. Phil's letter had said that her injured foot might not allow her to take the homeward journey for *ten* days. But that was unthinkable! She *must* come back before then. She must come back *before October 1st* when Rex and his mother arrived at Tilbury.

In spite of the fact that it was a cool day, Sally felt that she was bathed in perspiration. She could not stop trembling. Her nerves had always been good but this affair was bad enough to shake the strongest nerves. She was in a net which seemed to be closing more tightly about her every moment.

She made another journey out of the house, this time to a post office, and sent a frantic wire to the Villa at Etoile-sur-Mer.

'Grave risk of discovery imperative you return immediately even with bad foot. – SALLY.'

Yes, what did the bad foot matter? Phil could be lifted into train or boat or aeroplane. And once here she could pretend that she had had an accident in town, anything, in order to explain the injury to Martin.

Such a summons as that would, surely, bring Phil back at once, Sally told herself. And having sent it she felt better. But it was not a very happy day. Her mind seethed with thoughts of Rex and the unexpected inheritance and the fact that he was coming back meaning to marry her, and ... seethed with memories of last night. Oh, if she could blot out those memories just for a single moment! But she would go on remembering until she died.

Hour after hour she was tortured by the thought of Martin and her coming separation from him.

She did not see him all day. She wanted to. She needed badly the strengthening clasp of his hand and that look in his eyes which electrified her whole body. But he was out to lunch. He had left a message with Denham to say that after his massage he was going to have an eye-test at Dacre Cheniston's place, and would probably stay to lunch with him.

Sally lunched alone and felt more depressed than she had ever been in her life. She thought of Martin at the Chenistons; thought of pretty, dark-eyed Jan and that baby-boy who was Martin's god-son. How passionately she envied Jan with the husband and child who were all the world to her!

Some people were put into this world to be happy. Some seemed to make a muddle of things from the very beginning and to meet one difficulty after another. Sally was beginning to feel that she belonged to that tribe, but, of course, she could only blame herself for a great deal of this present disaster. She had been quite content in past days leading her simple existence and had been moderately satisfied with Rex as a future husband.

It was since she had stepped into Philippa's shoes that disaster had befallen her. Since then that she had learned how much she lacked and what love could really be. But for this whom could she blame save herself? Not that that made it any easier to bear.

In the midst of all her anxiety to-day she was also a little perplexed by Martin's conduct. Last night he had seemed so wholly in love; could not bear her out of his sight. To-day he was off hand, even avoided her. She could not begin to understand why. She could only take it for granted that he was behaving like any ordinary husband and that Phil would not have thought twice about it. But she was a love sick little fool. And for that sickness which people called 'love' there seemed no cure, no release.

To make the day more unpleasant, Philip Frankham called at the house soon after three and insisted upon seeing her. When Denham first brought her his card she sent down a message that she was 'not at home', but he sent back the message that it was 'urgent'. By that Sally deduced that Major Frankham intended to extract his pound of flesh and get something in return for the money expended on Philippa. Thoroughly disheartened, but afraid to refuse in case the man was cad enough to send those letters to Martin, Sally saw Philip in the library.

He was very debonair in grey flannels, with a rose in his buttonhole and sleekly brushed hair. All smiles he greeted her, bowing from the waist.

'Lovely as ever! Lovely and cruel. Why turn me down in the first place, little Phil?'

Sally shrugged her shoulders with a hopeless gesture. She was in the mood this afternoon to snap out the truth, tell this man that she was *not* 'little Phil' and that she found him nauseating. She caught sight of her reflection in the Queen Anne mirror beside which she was standing. She felt far from lovely, but, of course, she knew that no one could find fault with her appearance, so perfect was the cut of that golden brown chiffon velvet suit, delicate suède gloves, sable tie, and tiny Marina hat to match, perched so alluringly over one eyebrow. She had put on hat and gloves deliberately that she might pretend to Philip Frankham that she was going out.

'I haven't much time,' she told him. 'I'm due at a party in ten minutes.'

'So early?'

'Bridge,' said Sally. She had never played bridge in her life and never intended to.

Frankham half closed his eyes, strolled up to her and put a hand on her shoulder with an intimate, possessive gesture.

'Oh-h,' he drawled. 'The bridge isn't as important as all that, is it? Much better come along with me. We'll drive out of town if you like. What about tea down at Skindles?'

She moved away from him, hating his touch.

'I can't let my hostess down when I've promised to play bridge.'

'Who is it?'

Sally searched desperately in her mind for a name.

'Lady Bingham.'

Philip's lips curved unpleasantly.

'You're a liar, my sweet. The Binghams are out of town.'

The colour burnt Sally's cheeks.

'Well, I don't want to go out with you this afternoon. Can't you see that?'

'I may see it but I don't intend to accept it.'

'But you're incredible!' flashed Sally. 'If a woman wants to finish an affair…'

'And might I ask,' he broke in, 'what the said little woman does when she has written such letters as yours…?'

Sally thought:

'"Little woman!" God, how awful he is! This is really unbearable. Lord alone knows what Phil is going to do with this man when she does come back. I must keep him quiet for two or three days, until she comes … how horrible it is … my poor Martin…'

'Come,' said Frankham lazily. 'I can't think what's changed you so, Phil. We used to have fine times together.'

'I've had a lot to do and think about.'

'All excuses, my dear.'

'What do you want?'

'This,' he said, and pulled her into his arms.

Her body went stiff with sheer repugnance. He kissed her on the lips. Catching fire from the soft sweetness of her mouth, he kissed her again.

She wanted to die of shame. She had never hated anybody more violently. She put up a clenched fist and was on the point of striking him, but he caught the little fist and kissed it, laughing.

'A touch of your old spirit, my darling. Do you remember that day you lost your little temper after the polo and hit me, and then kissed the place to make it better?'

She remained speechless. Her lips were red lines of mutiny, her eyes blazing. Frankham whispered:

'Going to hit me now and then kiss the place to make it better?'

Still laughing, he bent his lips to hers again. It was at that instant the library door opened and Martin came in. Frankham did not see him because he had his back to the door. But Sally saw the tall thin figure, drooping slightly on the two sticks, and caught a glimpse of Martin's face. His expression was one of bitter disgust. She gasped:

'Martin!'

'What's that?' asked Frankham, and swung

round. The library door closed. 'Who was that?'

'Martin!' said Sally, panting. 'And he saw us. You cad!'

Frankham tugged at his collar. Then he pulled out a cigarette case.

'Don't pretend to be so upset. You never used to care what your husband thought of you. Look here, Phil...'

But Sally had gone. She had run out of the room and slammed the door behind her. The noise reverberated through the big house. Philip Frankham raised his brows, brushed back his hair, flicked an imaginary speck of dust from his coat sleeve, and with a not very pleasant smile, strolled to the front door.

14

Martin was half-way up the stairs when Sally reached him. Slowly, in the laborious fashion in which he had walked since his accident, he was climbing the stairs one by one, using both stick and banisters. As Sally reached him, he turned and looked at her unsmilingly. She thought she had never seen more complete scorn in the eyes of any man. It made her shrink. She could sympathise with him, but it was the most unjust thing in the world, she told herself, that Martin should imagine that *she* could do such a thing to him ... cheapen herself in the embrace of another man ... after last night.

'Martin...' she began.

'Don't speak to me,' he said.

She put a hand to her throat. A tiny anguished pulse seemed to be beating there.

'Martin, please...'

His bright contemptuous gaze swept her from head to foot. He was thinking how lovely she looked in that brown velvet suit with the mandarin hat on the ash blonde of her curls. Lovely and heartless and utterly bad. In a completely different light he thought of her now. She was not just Sally Browning who had masqueraded in Philippa's shoes for mercenary motives. She was rotten to the core. Her surrender of last night had not been born of mere generosity. She had extracted some excitement from it for herself. And she allowed that insufferable fellow, Frankham, to make love to her almost in the same breath. Had Philippa, his wife, behaved in a like manner with Frankham? Martin did not know. He felt too sick at heart to care. Sick and scornful of both these women who had betrayed him.

All that day he had been miserable, trying to readjust his emotions and recover his mental balance. For hours he had brooded over the affair and still could not see straight or make up his mind what best to do.

But, as the day lengthened, he had known beyond doubt that he still loved Sally Browning. That was the hardest part of it. To return home and find her in another man's arms was not the best thing that could have happened under the circumstances. It was probably the worst. Martin knew that it roused the worst in him, made him long to hurt this girl as she had never been hurt before.

'Martin, I … I didn't want that to happen… I was fighting against that foul man when you came in,' said Sally in an almost beseeching voice.

He laughed shortly.

'Do you think I care what you do? Go back to him and carry on with the good work,' he answered.

Sally looked as though he had hit her.

'But you don't really think…'

'I'm not concerned with what you do. I've had a busy day. I'm tired and going up to rest,' was his curt reply.

She caught his arm.

'Oh, please!…'

'My dear Phil…' The old name slipped out. He was so used to calling her that, and even now that he *knew* it was still easy… 'Don't be dramatic. It bores me. You can do exactly what you like, only leave me alone.'

He shook her hand off, turned and continued his difficult ascent of the staircase.

Wide-eyed, Sally stared after him. This was too horrible. He really imagined that she had welcomed and accepted Frankham's caresses. If only he had known how she loathed the man and detested the whole situation. Lost, indeed, was the lovely dream of yesterday. This was where her punishment began. Already she must shoulder some of the blame that was not hers but Phil's. Martin despised her. She felt that she had made a frightful mess of things. She had wanted to help Martin and help her cousin and she was only landing them both into greater difficulties.

She waited until Martin was out of sight, then mounted the stairs to the boudoir. Her eyes were dry and burning. She took off the hat and velvet coat, walked into her bedroom, locked the door, and then flung herself face downwards on the bed. For a very long while she lay there silent and tearless, but her body shook from head to foot.

This wild love for Martin was positively rending her in twain.

'It's more than I can stand,' she thought. 'Thank God I've wired for Phil. She *must* come back.'

And when Phil did come back, there could be nothing ahead for her, Sally, but unhappiness and regret in its most bitter form. Regret not that she had helped and comforted Martin and given all that she had to give, but that she was also instrumental in hurting him. Through endless time she must picture his unhappiness with Phil and suffer with and for him. As for Rex and their future … nothing was left of that. She dared not picture her forthcoming meeting with Rex. Misery, misery for all of them!

Vera came to her mistress's door, found it locked, and knocked.

There came Sally's muffled voice:

'I'm resting … what is it?'

Vera apologised and returned to the servants' hall to report that 'something was up'. 'Her ladyship' was in a mood and locked in her room, Major Frankham had just left the house, and the poor doctor was, according to Watson, 'prostrate in his room'. 'Her ladyship' wasn't as good and sweet as she had seemed of late, in Vera's opinion, and this was one of these 'human triangles' that folks saw at the pictures.

The next time Vera went to Mrs Frome's room it was half past six and time for her to dress. And there was a telegram for her.

Sally opened that telegram. She dismissed Vera who was watching her curiously, then, feeling her knees weak beneath her, Sally dropped into a chair and with an incredulous look on her face, re-read that wire. It staggered her. It had obviously been sent off before Philippa received Sally's summons. It said:

'Foot better. So long as you are all right don't want to hurry back. Leaving immediately for Spain and Gib. and coming back by water. Should reach England first week of October. Will wire you from boat. Carry on. No use writing me now as will be wandering.'

The long, extravagant telegram was unsigned. But Sally knew well who it was from. Aghast, she read it again and again until it was made clear to her.

Phil had left Etoile-sur-Mer. She would

never receive that imperative order to return at once, and it was useless trying to get in touch with her because she was 'wandering'. In her selfish, inconsequent fashion, hoping and believing that everything was all right and the position safe in Sally's hands, she had chosen to take a return journey which would last nearly a fortnight. Snatching another two weeks with her lover. Pleasant, thrilling days in Spain, and then on board ship from Gibraltar.

Sally began to laugh hysterically to herself. She crumpled the wire in her hand, covered her face and went on laughing until laughter changed to tears. This was too much for anybody to bear. The masquerade was going to end in tragedy. Everything had gone wrong. What utter fools she and Phil had been ever to imagine that it could go right. It was mostly Phil's fault ... she had had no right to do this thing. She could have nobody but herself to blame if she came back and found catastrophe awaiting her.

Sally moaned to herself:

'What can I do?'

There was absolutely nothing to be done except to sit and wait for the avalanche which would fall and bury them all. It was not humanly possible for her to find Phil and get her back, neither was it possible for her to stop Rex and his mother from arriving and descending upon her. This, of course, was the final blow. She had fully expected Phil to be back before the end of the week. She had intended to be back at the Bayswater boarding-house as Sally Browning before Rex arrived.

Now she must stay here and heaven alone knew how she was going to handle the situation in its present form. The one thing that stood out in her mind was that she must spare Martin. She *must not* let Martin guess that she was Sally, and that his wife was abroad with her lover.

For a long time she sat there, huddled, crying rather like a lost, bewildered child. But at last she roused herself. She must dress for dinner. She must carry on. It was no use giving in till the end came. She had no real hope of sparing Martin now, but she was going to try. The great thing would be to keep Rex and Martin apart.

While she bathed and dressed, utterly disconsolate, she remembered this afternoon's unfortunate incident. Martin's disillusion was only just beginning, she thought miserably. What could she do to make him happy again? When she had spoken to him on the stairs he had looked so bitter and so changed from the happy Martin of yesterday.

She might be able to make him believe in her if she tried very hard. She might be able to erase from his mind the memory of Philip Frankham. But having wooed him back to her arms, she dared not hold him there. *Dared not* ... for all their sakes.

Was ever anybody in such a quandary?

She put on a black dinner dress, dusted a little rouge powder into her cheeks. They were so pale. She was losing more and more of her tan and not looking anything like as well as when she had returned from South Africa. The strain had left a mark on her. But there was an ethereal quality about her beauty which was new and alluring.

Nobody was more conscious of it than Martin when he saw her that night. At first he had decided to stay in bed and have a tray brought to him. But he had been too restless to lie there, and afraid of a sleepless night. In spite of all the little bottles in that enamelled cupboard down in his consulting room he was not a man who would ever take drugs. But never had Martin Frome been greater in need of drugs than tonight. His nerves were in pieces. His thoughts revolved in ceaseless confusion around Sally Browning and his wife.

The thing that made him most savage, was the very knowledge that he could not stop loving *Sally*, whatever she had done to him, the allure of her was in his very blood now for good and all. He was almost ashamed of his intense feeling for her. He told himself that it was obvious that she was no good. This afternoon's incident was small, really,

243

compared to the tremendous wrong which she had done him in taking his wife's place. And yet it stung more badly than any of the other things. That was sheer primitive jealousy, and he knew it. And it was that which made him most ashamed.

Cheniston had given him a good report about his eyes. The optic nerves had almost totally recovered and there was nothing for him to worry about. Despite the shock of this morning he was using his limbs better; the masseur had been pleased. There was no doubt about his future recovery and return to work. That was fairly certain now. Pretty wonderful when he thought of the long days on his back when one or two of his colleagues had as good as admitted that he was done for. Well, he still owed that much to Sally. Undoubtedly she had helped him back to health. But he asked himself savagely what the hell was the good of making him well again only to destroy all his desire for existence?

He let Watson help him dress and then joined Sally in the dining-room.

The meal was not a happy one. For the butler's benefit they talked. Martin, in somewhat indifferent voice, discussed topical subjects. Sally answered politely. But she felt horribly nervous and wretched. He refused to meet her eye. Only when she was not looking at him he shot a quick glance at her, stared a moment almost resentfully at the pale gold satin gleam of back and shoulders under the black veil of the little chiffon cape she was wearing, then at the fair pretty head. The faint dusting of rouge on her cheeks misled him. The colour looked natural in the glow of candlelight. He took it for granted that that warm rosy flush sprang from thoughts of her lover. Frankham was her lover. Or a dozen other men. How did he know? She might be capable of anything.

During that meal he was more than ever struck by the incredibility of the whole situation. He asked himself:

'Is this all a bad dream … is this really Phil … is there such a person as Sally?'

The meal over, they went to the library for coffee. Every day now the weather grew cooler. A fire burned warmly to dispel the chill and gloom of the big room. As Martin settled himself in his usual chair and laid aside his sticks, he glanced at the favourite painting of Philippa's mother with the child in her arms. The very similarity between that tender mother-figure and this girl enraged him. Family likeness, eh? That woman was Sally's aunt. They were all alike, *damn them!*

Sally, lighting a cigarette, stole a glance at Martin and saw the peculiar expression on his face. That mouth of his, usually humorous and sympathetic, was a savage line. His eyes were burning.

Her heart sank yet lower. What had happened now? Was he just furious about Philip Frankham? Had that incident destroyed all his peace and happiness? If he felt like this, what, in heaven's name, would he feel when he knew about Phil?

Sally was in anguish. There was no desire in her heart to-night save to bring back peace to *him*.

When Denham had cleared away the coffee she deliberately broke through the hostility of the formal atmosphere between them. She said:

'Martin, please don't go on being angry or … disgusted. If you will only take my word I can assure you that I detest that man and that what happened was entirely against my will.'

Martin stared at the cigar which he was smoking.

'Sorry, I don't believe you.'

'But why? Why shouldn't you?'

Almost it was on the tip of his tongue to say:

'Because *I know*, you little fool. I know the whole monstrous plan that you and Phil between you organised in order to make hell on earth for me.'

But he checked himself. Not yet would he let that truth be known to Sally. He was tortured and he wanted to torture her. He wondered how far he could hurt her before he wrung an admission of facts from *her.*

'Why don't you go out?' he rapped.

'I don't want to.'

'No gigolos handy?'

She flushed scarlet.

'Martin!'

'Oh well, don't let it upset you. I can't believe that you worry one way or the other what I think of you or what I know about you.'

Her heart jerked uneasily.

'Why do you say that?'

'Never mind.'

That drained the colour from her cheeks. And for the first time there flashed into her brain the question.

'Does he know?'

The next moment Martin deliberately dispelled that fear for her. He talked to her exactly as though she was his wife.

'My dear Phil, you must think me quite a fool not to realise that you've had a motive in being so charming to me lately. It's a very good screen for your activities with other men – and...'

'Oh!' came from her in a long-drawn breath.

'And of course, a way of substantiating the bank balance. You know I wasn't born yesterday, my child.'

He wondered how she would take that. And it almost pleased him because she

247

flinched so perceptibly. Something was to be said for her that she could look ashamed even if she did not feel it. But just how ashamed she was, Martin did not begin to understand.

Sally wanted to sink through the floor. She wanted to cover her burning face with her hands and fly from the room, weeping. Phil deserved such words, but she ... however wrong she had been to take part in this masquerade, she had never swerved one instant from her devotion and her love for Martin.

He stuck the cigar between his teeth.

'Would another hundred or so be useful?'

'Don't!' was wrung from her. 'Please don't!'

'Ah! You don't want it. Got plenty at the moment. Well, my sweet Phil, you thanked me last night most charmingly. I'd be almost prepared to part with a few more hundreds for such thanks.'

She stood before him like a frozen creature. She said in a stricken voice:

'I would never, never have thought that *you* could be ... so *beastly*.'

'Women can make beasts of the nicest husbands, my dear. Women like yourself, for instance.'

Her heart seemed to knock and hurt. She turned so pale that he thought she was going to faint. He wondered why it should distress her so that he behaved like a beast. But he was really conscious of nothing to-night but that fierce wish to hurt her. The pain in his own heart was so intolerable. And he loved her. He knew that as he looked at her. He wondered why any woman with so divine a face and form should be given such an unscrupulous character. Then she whispered:

'I'm sorry. If you won't believe me, I can't *make you*. But you're wrong if you think I want any gigolo or any lover.'

'Still in love with your husband?' he asked with sarcasm.

Wild tears stung her eyelids as she answered:

'I do … love … *you!*'

He could almost have killed her then. She said those words with a sincerity that might have deceived the most doubtful man. Yet how could he be deceived, knowing who she was and what she had done? Suddenly he put up a hand, caught her wrist and pulled her down to him.

'Do you? *Do you?*'

She collapsed in that embrace and sobbed desperately against his shoulder. The black chiffon cape fell to the floor. Her bare smooth arms circled his neck. With a wet cheek pressed to his she said:

'Don't be angry with me any more. Oh, don't!'

How well now he knew that this was not his wife. Phil's reaction to a row was utterly different. If he snapped, she would snap back; if he criticised, she would tell him what thought of him. But this girl, shivering, weeping in his arms, she was different. The confusion in Martin's brain intensified and caused a mental disturbance which he could barely control. He could not comprehend why Sally should cry and cling to him, unless it was that she was afraid. Did she regret her generosity of yesterday? Was she terrified now that he was going to make further demands on her?

With every drop of blood in his body he wanted to take the grace and beauty of this girl, Sally, and hold it against the world; tell her that he knew everything but he didn't care, he only wanted her, her for eternity.

He found himself covering the fair shining head with wild kisses that drifted down to her wet cheeks and burned against the shivering flame of her lips. He said:

'Shall I forget what I saw this afternoon, my sweet? Shall I just remember last night – and you? Are you going to show me how much you do love me, you lovely thing!'

Suddenly she ceased weeping and clinging and grew cold, stiff in his embrace. Like a black cloud there descended upon her the memory of who and what she was. Hadn't she told herself earlier to-day that there could never be a repetition of last night? Hadn't her conscience been pricking her all day, reminding her of the principles and ethics upon which she had been brought up? Hadn't she known, oh, even in the hours of surrender, that she had had no right! It had been unfair to them all The temptation was terrific because the main desire in her heart was to give to *him*. Isn't that the desire at the back of every woman's love; the fount from which springs all her passion, her loving?

But even for Martin she could not and must not do this.

Intently he watched her, saw the change that came over her.

'What is it?' he asked.

In panic she slid from his arms and stood before him, breathing fast, smoothing back her tumbled curls.

'I … I don't feel well…'

He sat back in his chair, griping the arms with his hands. A cynical smile curved his mouth. He thought he understood. She was not so anxious, after all, to pay the price for her position in this house.

'It's a very sudden illness, isn't it, darling?'

'I … I've had a bad head all day.'

'As bad as that? Can't the doctor prescribe?'

She avoided his gaze.

'I'll be all right. I … think I'll go to bed.'

'I'll come and say good night.'

Her cheeks burned and paled again. If he knew how he was torturing her! But she tried, desperately, to stick to the course she had mapped out for herself, the one course which she believed to be right.

'I'll say good night *now*,' came from her, almost inaudibly.

Then Martin said:

'My dear Phil, how transparent you are.'

'You think...' she began.

'I think I know how you feel. You do nothing without a motive, and I suppose there's nothing for you to gain by being charming to-night.'

She could only look at him speechlessly. Then she turned and walked out of the room and shut the door.

Martin put the cigar between his teeth again but almost immediately took it out and flung it savagely into the fire. He let his head fall between his hands. He said to himself:

'I won't be able to go on like this. Soon I shall have to tell her that I know. It's only a question of who breaks first ... Sally or me.'

15

Those days preceding the first of October were nothing short of a nightmare for Sally.

Phil was lost, either wandering about Spain or at Gibraltar or on the sea, Sally did not know which. Rex and his mother were drawing ever nearer and nearer Tilbury.

Martin behaved in a peculiar fashion which Sally failed to understand, although never once did she imagine that he had discovered the whole subterfuge.

He alternated between being icy, sarcastic, almost hostile; and passionately demanding. When he was the former she was bewildered and miserable. When he was the latter she was agonised with the desire to surrender, but controlled it knowing that she would be utterly wrong to do otherwise.

She was tortured. But that Martin knew that, and was even deliberately the instigator of her mental agony, she never guessed. She could not account for his treatment of her save that he was thoroughly disgusted at her supposed 'affair' with Philip Frankham.

Frankham wrote or telephoned every day. With every communication from him there was a veiled threat. She temporised desperately, trying not to be too bitterly insulting in case his temper got the better of him and he sent Phil's foolish letters to Martin. All day long it seemed to her that she waged a secret battle for Martin ... endeavoured to spare him. But the contest was an uneven one and she felt that she was losing.

She was thankful that he appeared interested in the hospital and spent much of his time amongst his colleagues. He had even consented to act as consultant on one or two occasions where his opinion was invaluable.

And Sally, lost and lonely, wandered about the big house or accepted invitations to parties which she found boring and futile, in order to keep up her reputation as Mrs Martin Frome.

Twice Martin came to her room 'to say good night'. And she had to pretend either that she was asleep, or tired or 'not in the mood'. It broke her heart because invariably such an excuse drew forth sarcasm from him which filled her with burning shame. It as so unjust. And the thing was no less tolerable because she had committed the fatal mistake of falling in love with him.

Then came the morning of October the first when Sally woke out of a fevered, restless sleep to face the fact that to-day she must meet Rex's boat at Tilbury.

Everything conspired to make things difficult for her. Martin was inclined to be friendly to-day. He had even his kind, humorous smile for her when she said good morning to him, and there was something almost wistful in his voice when he said:

'It's a lovely day, my dear. One of those real golden October mornings. I'll chuck playing round my job and you break your various appointments, and let's take that trip to Devonshire that Stenning recommended.'

Sally gave a nervous smile.

'I – it sounds good ... lovely ... but I ... I'm really rather busy just at the moment.'

Martin lit a cigarette carefully, avoiding her eye. He was sitting in his chair in front of the library fire. For a long while he had been feeling a complete dislike of London and Harley Street and this big house. He wanted to get into the country, to breathe sweet fresh air into his lungs. He wanted to forget all his crashing disappointments and troubles, if only for a few days. He wanted to forget Phil, his wife, and the impending disaster connected with her and above all, he wanted to forget that Sally had wronged him, and to remember only that she was lovely and could be kind and that he was eaten up with love for her. A love that was as mad, as intense, as foolish as a boy's.

So she was tired of being kind, he thought ironically. This Sally, with her grey, limpid eyes and sweet, beguiling mouth, was full of secret motives. Her inner consciousness was dark with intrigue and for reasons of her own she did not want to go away and play the dutiful wife. She was busy in town! What about? Who with?

Martin felt a sudden stubborn wish to enforce upon her those duties and responsibilities which she had so lightly taken over from Phil. He said:

'Run along and tell Vera to pack for you. We're going out of town this morning, my child.'

Sally's face went quite white.

'It's impossible!' she said.

The Shipping Office had told her that the *Angerry Castle* docked at mid-day. Rex would be expecting her to meet him there when he landed. And if he didn't find her waiting, he would go straight to her rooms in Bayswater. Then he would discover that she hadn't been living there for the last month. But he would know where to find her. Just before he left South Africa, he would have got her first letter telling him of her 'job' as secretary to her cousin, Mrs Frome. He would come straight here and ask for Miss Browning and be told that she was not here and never had been. And after that, chaos!

In panic-stricken silence, Sally stared at Martin.

He took the cigarette from his mouth. The humour and kindness was wiped from his face as though by a sponge. He could see that Sally was frightened. There was something behind her fear that he did not know, of course. Probably a thousand things that he did not know.

He looked at her bitterly. She wore a dark tailored suit and a little high-necked jumper of fleecy wool, primrose-hued. She seemed young in that yellow jumper, almost like a schoolgirl. Young and innocent and fair. Martin Frome loved and hated her in the same breath. But he was determined not to spare her to-day.

'There's no appointment you can't break, my dear Phil. You run along and do a little of that telephoning you're so fond of, and tell Vera to pack. We might take your little car and you shall drive.'

She put a hand to her throat. She felt that she was being cornered. She couldn't drive a car. That was out of the question.

'I don't want to drive,' she said. 'I find it too tiring.'

'That's very unlike you. You used to adore driving.'

'I don't now.'

'Very changeable, aren't you? I've never met anybody who alters so from one minute to the next.'

Something seemed to choke in her throat. 'I'm ... sorry.'

'No matter. Have the big car if you like.

257

We'll go down in the Daimler.'

He saw that she was shaking now. He wondered why she was so perturbed. She said:

'Honestly, Martin, I don't want to go to Devonshire to-day.'

He fixed her with a penetrating gaze.

'Why?'

'I tell you … I've got appointments I can't break.'

'With one of your gigolos?'

'Oh, don't be so ridiculous!'

'Is Frankham taking you out to dinner?'

'No, I haven't seen Major Frankham this week and I don't want to see him.'

'Then what's keeping you in town?'

'Must I explain every little thing that I do?'

'I seem to remember a moment when you murmured something about adoring me and living for me alone.'

That brought the hot carnation pink to her cheeks, to her throat, scorching her.

She made no answer, only turned her head away, and wondered what in heaven's name she was going to do if Martin persisted in this mood to-day. Oh, mad, mad she had been ever to let him see that she adored him. And her love for him was gnawing at her, urging her to throw herself into his arms and beg him to take her with him everywhere, anywhere, so long as he loved her again.

She made a desperate attempt to ape her

cousin Philippa. She even snapped:

'Don't nag me, Martin. Let me do what I want.'

He thought:

'You're afraid of me, petrified with fear, in fact. But it's too late for you to try Phil's gambit. I'm not going to let you win the game so easily...'

Aloud he said:

'It's high time you did what *I* want, Phil. You're getting thoroughly spoiled, my sweet. No more arguing. Run along and pack.'

In dismay she stared at him. As if she hadn't found things trying enough as it was, without Martin suddenly turning round and becoming a tyrant. She could not blame him. She knew perfectly well that he was fully justified in taking up such an attitude after the years he had spent with Phil.

Breathlessly she said:

'Why don't you go to Devonshire by yourself? I – I'll follow.'

'Charming of you, my sweet, but I thought your one wish was to look after your poor sick husband.'

'I do want to look after you.'

'Right. Then run along and pack.'

Mutely she walked out of the room. And Martin looked after her with his brooding gaze. He had won the day – but it was a poor victory and he felt nothing but apprehension. He wondered just why she was so loth to accompany him. Perhaps Phil was due back at any minute? Perhaps Sally was in a fix of some kind. Well, let her get on with it. He was not going to move one muscle to help her. When the final storm burst he would get the worst of it and he felt sorrier for himself than for anybody. He could not be sorry for Philippa. Her conduct had been altogether too infamous, and he was not going to allow himself to feel one ounce of pity for Sally, or let her strange, undeniable allure soften him.

Sally went to her room and faced the fact that she was nicely caught. She had no alternative but to accompany Martin to Devonshire. If she persisted in her refusal, it would look so odd that she would undoubtedly give away the whole situation. And it was a little late for her to start imitating Phil too closely now, considering that she had been so attentive to Martin all these weeks. It must look most odd to him that she should not jump at the chance of taking him down to Devonshire where the sunshine and the change of air might complete his recovery.

Sally's brow was damp with perspiration as she gave Vera the order to pack. This was all Phil's fault. How *dared* Phil travel so far afield and insist upon staying away just to satisfy her base, selfish motives!

And now what was Sally to do about Rex and Mrs Trencham? Martin wanted to leave

London in an hour's time. And in two hours Rex would land at Tilbury.

There was only one thing that she could do and she set to it with the utmost reluctance. She sat down and wrote a somewhat incoherent letter to Rex, telling him that she had found that she had made a mistake and must break her engagement and that she thought it better not to see him again.

'It is not that I am going to marry anybody else; in fact, my life will be quite difficult and lonely, but I do not think it would be fair to either of us to go through with the plans we originally made. You have plenty of money now and will doubtless find somebody who will make you a very good wife. Please, please forgive me, Rex. When I promised to marry you I was too young and inexperienced to realise what I was doing, but I know now that we should never have been happy together.

'It will save so much pain on both sides if we don't meet again.'

'Ever yours,
'SALLY.'

Having written this note, Sally slipped her engagement ring into the envelope and sealed it.

She thought how dreadful it was that it mattered so little to her to part with that pearl ring and all that it symbolised. Yet she had told Rex the truth in saying that she had been too inexperienced to know what she was doing when she had promised to marry him. He had been her first suitor, her first emotional experience. And she had been lonely and bored. What a terrible mistake it was for girls to tie themselves up under such circumstances! And how utterly different the real thing was when it came along! Sally knew that now to her bitter cost.

She could only console herself with the thought that she was not mortally hurting Rex. He was not the type to take such a blow very badly. He was too self-contained and practical. He might even feel that he was well out of it, and, of course, his mother would be delighted to have her son to herself again.

Sally took a taxi round to the Bayswater boarding-house and left the note with Miss Pouting. A Mr Trenchman would call for it, probably that morning, she told the woman, and then rushed back to Harley Street.

She had the fatalistic feeling that this was, indeed, the beginning of the end when at length she sat in the big Daimler beside Martin, and Smith wrapped the rug round them both, and they moved off for their 'holiday'.

She was in deeper waters now than she could swim. She was just drowning, while those waters swirled over her helpless head. She could do nothing to avert the catastrophe when it finally came. But she wanted to make a final effort to save Martin from the disclosure of Phil's infidelities.

Sally knew that Phil was due back in England in about two or three days' time, and would probably telephone home at once, discover that she was in Devonshire with Martin and wait for a communication from her. So Sally had left a message with Vera that should a 'Miss Maxwell' telephone, she was to be told to write to Mrs Frome at the Palace Hotel, Torquay.

Martin had wired for rooms.

'The Palace is a grand spot, with beautiful grounds. It used to be the Bishop of Exeter's Palace and was converted into a hotel. Dacre and Jan went down there last year and thoroughly enjoyed themselves,' was Martin's comment as they drove away from Harley Street. 'I'm damned glad to be rid of London, aren't you, Phil?'

Sally, with thoughts of Rex and what he would say and do when he got her letter tormenting her, only answered vaguely. A horrible thought had just leapt to her mind. Supposing Rex refused to accept his *congé* and went round to Harley Street and demanded to see her. Then he would be told that Mrs Frome had no secretary. That would make him suspicious and he would decide to get in touch with 'Mrs Frome'. He might even follow her to Devonshire and demand to see her. And it would be more than she could do to face Rex and pretend that she *wasn't* Sally.

Martin glanced at the girl beside him. She looked pale and preoccupied but devilishly attractive, he told himself, with that brown velvet beret on the side of the blonde head, and the rich beauty of Philippa's sables circling her throat.

What was she thinking about? What was worrying her? Of course, she was not looking forward to this holiday. She didn't care a damn about him. She was only annoyed because she had been forced to come with him. It hadn't taken her long to grow tired of being the ministering angel.

He knew that if he was lover-like it would distress her. But he did not want to spare her. Yet he loved her with every drop of blood in his body, and that was the terrible tragedy of the whole affair.

He put out a hand and took one of hers, toying idly with the slender fingers in the delicate suède gloves.

'I think we should make this our second honeymoon, don't you, my sweet?'

She kept her gaze straight ahead of her and answered only by a faint shrug of the shoulders. She knew perfectly well that the mere clasp of his hand and that tone in his voice made her heart beats quicken breathlessly. But that was what she must control. And she could only foresee a scene this evening – another of those scenes which would leave Martin bitter and bewildered and put her in the light of a selfish, ungenerous little beast who took everything from him and gave nothing in return, save when it suited her.

They left the tramlines and the busy thoroughfares of London and moved out on to the Great West Road. It was really a lovely day, this first day of October. The trees had discarded all their greenery and were burnt gold and russet brown. There was a slight chill in the air, but the sky was blue, and there was that brisk freshness of a fine autumn morning which is compensation for the end of the lazy warmth of summer.

It struck Sally more than once how intensely sad it was that this could not, in truth, have been a second honeymoon, and that things could not have been right between her and Martin. Bitterly sad for them both. Martin said:

'Why so depressed? Surely these appointments weren't so important as all that? Are you sulking because you've had to come out of town with me?'

Her fingers moved restlessly in his, but he held on to them with deliberation.

'I don't mind coming with you,' came

from her in a low voice.

'Thanks, my sweet,' he said, laughed, and sat back in his corner of the car. 'Well, you'll have to be a very good little wife for the next few days, because I've got no Watson to look after me.'

'I shall like looking after you.'

He wanted to say: 'That isn't true,' but held his peace. There were moments when Sally Browning seemed genuinely solicitous for him and quite sincere with her sympathy, her kindliness. An odd mixture, this girl ... a mixture of good and bad. And he loved her so much that he wished he had never set eyes on her. He had been happier leading that empty, one-sided existence with egotistical Phil, before he knew what the glory of loving really meant.

He was ashamed of his own nature.

'I shouldn't let this thing conquer me,' he told himself. 'It's a lack of intelligence for any man to allow a woman to dominate him so completely. I've got my life as a doctor and my work to go back to. I mustn't let this thing get me down.'

But it was getting him down and nobody knew it better than Martin. And for the next hour or two he relapsed into a gloomy silence which Sally made no effort to break.

They broke the journey at Bath. At the Grand Pump Hotel, Martin registered 'Mr and Mrs Martin Frome'. There was to be no 'scene' that night, because Martin booked two rooms, went straight to bed before dinner and stayed there. He seemed disinterested in Sally or how she, personally, spent the evening.

The truth was that Martin was a very tired man. He was still weak from his recent accident, and the mental strain through which he had passed this last few days had taken a toll of him. He was white and exhausted when they reached Bath, and that night seemed more like the earlier days when Sally had first taken her cousin's place. Martin was an invalid, to be taken care of, a small boy who needed mothering.

She saw, personally, that his hot water bottle was filled and that he was made comfortable with more pillows, because he liked sleeping high. She even folded his clothes for him, because there was no Watson to do it.

Martin watched from his bed, arms folded behind his head, his face a mask. It made her heart ache to look at him because there were such shadows under his eyes and he seemed to have grown suddenly thinner. She wondered, with a horrid twist of the heart, whether he had been doing too much and it had set him back. He was nothing like the buoyant, vital person that he had seemed those days preceding her complete surrender.

'Perhaps the odd way in which I am behaving has upset him,' she thought miserably. 'If only I could tell him how much he really means to me and how hopelessly my hands are tied!'

She busied herself in the room for a moment. Martin continued to watch her in silence. She had changed from her travelling suit into a grey chiffon dinner dress, and wore turquoise earrings and a long blue string of beads to match. She looked lovely, but she, too, was tired. He puzzled over her, alternating between contempt for what he knew she was, and pleasure in these little services which she rendered him. Strange unaccountable Sally! What could he make of her? Why, in God's name, did she bother about him at all?

She came to the foot of the bed.

'Is there anything more I can do for you?'

'Nothing, thanks.'

'I'll come up after dinner and make sure that they've sent your tray.'

'You needn't. I can ring if I want anything.'

She played nervously with her beads, her eyes full of barely concealed yearning.

'You're sure you won't want me again?'

'Sure.'

She glanced at the door which communicated with her own bedroom.

'I shall be there if you do need me in the night.'

'You needn't worry. I'm fagged out and I shall probably sleep the clock round.'

'You're not in any pain?'

'No. Only this hip aches sometimes when I've overtired.'

'Then I'll say good night, Martin.'

He dragged his gaze from the beauty of her. She had no right to wear that wistful, saint-like expression; no right at all. What did she want now, he asked himself savagely?

'Good night!' he almost snapped at her.

Without understanding what she had done to deserve the increased hostility from him, Sally went from the room and slowly shut the door.

She could not face a solitary meal in the hotel restaurant. So she went straight to her own room, had an omelette and a cup of coffee sent up to her, and lay in bed, trying to read a paper. She did not seem to have looked at the daily papers for days. War debates, politics, murders, divorces, all the dozen and one tragedies and sorrows that were reported, what interest had she in them? Her own tragedy was too imminent and too great. Her mind was full of Martin and of Phil. And she thought of Rex, too, and wondered what his reactions would be to that letter which she had left for him at the boarding-house.

The memory of Martin's tired, disillusioned face haunted her until she could scarcely bear it. God alone knew that she was thoroughly weary of the struggle and all the strain of this masquerade. But she would gladly have gone through any amount more if she could make Martin happy always.

She worried about his health, too. Late that night, still sleepless, she put on a dressing-gown, opened the communicating door and found the light still on in Martin's bedroom. He had fallen asleep with the table lamp burning beside him. She tiptoed to the bed and stood looking down at him a moment, her eyes full of grief. So young he looked, asleep like that, with dark hair ruffled and one arm flung across the pillow and brows knit as though in his slumber he was trying to solve some weighty problem.

'Oh, my dear,' she whispered. 'Oh, my dear, you'll never, never know how much I love you!'

She switched off the lamp, bent, put her lips against his hair, and left his room as soundlessly as she had entered it.

The moment the door closed, Martin's eyes opened. He stared in the direction of that door as though he could still see Sally's graceful figure in her velvet wrapper, with the fair curls falling loosely about her neck. And he thought:

'Why, in hell's name, should she kiss me like that? That isn't pretending. She *does* care about me in some funny way. I wish to

God I understood!'

For the next hour he could not sleep but lay brooding and worrying, troubled by the faint sound of weeping which came through that closed door.

16

They reached the Palace Hotel in Torquay in time for lunch. Under more normal circumstances, Sally would have taken considerable interest in the fine building and the wonderful grounds. They were full of the glory of autumn tints; vivid clusters of chrysanthemums, exotic dahlias, and the masses of Michaelmas daisies, palest mauve and darkest purple, in the flower beds which fringed the smooth green lawns.

Mr and Mrs Frome were given an attractive suite, and as soon as Sally had unpacked for herself and Martin, she wandered into the garden and found a point from which she could see the blue Devon sea which was like rippling azure silk against the red cliffs this sunlit October morning. The air was soft here – much warmer than in London. It was Sally's first introduction to Devonshire, and she might have been so happy here with *him!* But happiness seemed far distant from Sally.

Every moment was fraught with anxiety. She was wondering from one instant to the next when she would hear from Phil, or from Rex, or from both. The only thing she could be thankful for was that the 'second honeymoon' was not developing along the lines which she had expected. Martin seemed disinclined to be lover-like. He was morose and *distrait* and had little to say to her. She found herself longing passionately for the old charming companionship which had been theirs soon after she had installed herself in Philippa's place.

It was during that afternoon that the bombshell fell. Martin was in his room, resting. Sally sat in the lounge trying to read a book. She sensed that somebody was coming toward her and looked up. She saw a man in tweeds, carrying a Burberry. A broadly built man with curly hair, and a brick red skin, and horn-rimmed glasses. For an instant she sat quite paralysed. Her fingers became nerveless and she dropped the book. Then she sprang to her feet.

'Rex!' she said.

The man stood before her in silence for a moment, staring at her through his glasses. He was unsmiling. Then he flung his Burberry on to a chair and gave a brief laugh.

'So you *are* here, Sally!'

She had never felt more inclined to faint in her life. Her worst fears had been realised. Rex *had* followed. And now it seemed to her that the end was very near. She said in a smothered voice:

'I ... my dear Rex ... I didn't expect...' she

broke off, stammering, utterly at a loss for words.

'You didn't expect me,' he broke in. 'No, I don't suppose you did. But I'm not the man to be chucked in *that* off-hand fashion, I can assure you.'

'B-but you g-got my letter!'

'I got it all right, yesterday. A nice welcome it was, too. Honestly, Sally, you could have knocked me down with a feather. And mother was flabbergasted. She always had the highest opinion of you and so had I. It never entered my head that you were going to break with me in that brutal way.'

She looked at him with eyes of tragedy.

'I didn't mean to be brutal. I didn't want to be. One is forced into brutalities in this life.'

'Don't waste words. Let's have the truth from you. Why have you broken our engagement? You seemed perfectly satisfied with it when you left Jo'burg.'

'I found that I'd made a mistake, Rex. I thought it better to tell you.'

'A very sudden discovery, wasn't it?'

She sat down weakly on the arm of the chair.

'I suppose it was.'

'There's something more in it than you've told me and I want to know what it is.'

She shook her head.

'You shouldn't have come here. You'd have

done far better to do as I asked and not try and see me.'

'Hell to that. We were engaged, and why should you chuck me over all of a sudden and expect me to take it lying down?'

'Rex, I was very young when we first fixed things up and I hadn't had much experience of life. You'll admit that?'

'You were in love with me, weren't you?'

She looked at him almost pityingly. He cut rather a pitiful figure. There was no pride in Rex, only wounded vanity. He was a man with a very high opinion of himself. This had struck at his self-conceit. It had made him ridiculous in his mother's sight, too. Naturally Mrs Trenchman would never understand how any girl could jilt her precious boy, and she had probably been very biting about it and spurred Rex on until he shared her vindictive spirit.

'I *was* in love with you, Rex,' said Sally. 'But I've since discovered that it wasn't the real thing, that's all. Heaps of engagements end that way. I don't see why it should seems so strange to you.'

'You don't change unless you find somebody else. You've met another fellow. That's the honest truth, isn't it?'

She spread out a hand with a hopeless gesture.

'Well, supposing it is. That happens often, too. One does meet somebody else and discover that the first love was a mistake.'

'So you told me a lie.'

'What about?'

'You said in your letter it wasn't because you wanted to marry somebody else.'

'That's the truth. I'm not going to marry anybody else.'

Trenchman thrust his hands in his trousers pockets. He felt truculent, aggressive, and he looked it. And he stared resentfully at his former fiancée. Very expensively dressed in that smart blue jumper suit, and her velvet beret. He noticed the aquamarine ring which she wore in place of his pearl, too. Tremendously dolled up and damned pretty! He had to admit that he had never met a prettier girl than Sally. He would have been proud to introduce her to everybody as his wife. He was damned annoyed about this broken engagement. There were things he didn't understand about it either. He said:

'Well, why chuck me if you don't want to marry someone else? You got mother's letter about the money, didn't you? I'm a rich man.'

'I know, Rex,' said Sally gently. 'But that doesn't make any difference. I couldn't marry a man just because he had money.'

'Well, where's this other bloke and who is he?' asked Rex loudly.

Sally looked around the lounge in terror. At any moment, Martin might come down

276

from his rest. She wondered what, in heaven's name, to do and how to prevent the two men from meeting. Rex added:

'And what is all this funny stuff about you leaving the boarding-house and only calling for your letters, and being secretary to your cousin Philippa? When I got that letter I told mother I wasn't going to accept my *congé* until I'd seen you. There's a good deal that needs explanation. I went round to Dr Frome's house and they told me that no Miss Browning lived there and that Mrs Frome hadn't a secretary. The butler said I'd better ask Mrs Frome. I had a feeling that you'd be here. So I hired a car and drove down. But why all the secrecy?'

Sally put a hand to her head. She was utterly stumped for a reply. She did not want to tell Rex the truth. She could not risk him attacking Martin, and yet if Martin appeared, the fat would be in the fire.

'Why don't you say something?' demanded Rex in his most bullying voice.

She could only look at him dumbly and wonder how she had ever imagined herself in love with this man.

Then all the colour drained from her cheeks. The doors of the lift had opened and a man was emerging slowly on two sticks. Martin, just as she had anticipated, was coming down to tea.

She no longer felt panic-stricken. Her feelings became so acute that they had a numbing effect. She sat like a frozen creature, just staring at Martin, and thought:

'This is the end!'

Rex followed her gaze.

'Who's this on the sticks? Someone you know?'

Somehow Sally managed to whisper:

'That is … Martin Frome.'

Martin approached Sally and the red-faced, broad-shouldered man who looked as though he had just come from the Colonies. Martin presumed that Sally had found one of the hotel visitors to talk to. But the man in tweeds immediately addressed him:

'Good afternoon, Dr Frome. I hope you don't mind my coming down like this, but I wanted to speak to your wife's secretary. At least she says she's her secretary, although they didn't seem to know at your house that she was down here. They said you and Mrs Frome were alone. My name's Trencham. Miss Browning and I are engaged to be married. At least we were, but she appears to have broken it off. I–'

He stopped. Something in Sally's appearance stopped him. She looked ghastly and she was swaying as though she was going to faint.

Then Martin said:

'Look out! Catch her!'

The last thing which Sally realised before

she lost consciousness was that Rex put an arm about her and prevented her from falling to the ground.

Martin was shaken. But his quick brain had summed up the situation. Sally Browning had been engaged and this was her fiancé. Doubtless the poor fellow was as bewildered as everybody else and had been in his turn deceived and badly treated. Martin was a little sorry for him. But if Sally wished to terminate her engagement, that was none of his business. At the same time there was a queer spark of jealousy in Martin. He could not look with indifference upon any man who wanted to possess Sally and he knew it. He said tersely:

'Put her in that chair. Go and fetch some brandy...'

Rex deposited Sally's inert form in the armchair by the fire. Fortunately there were few people in the lounge because it was not yet the tea hour and many of the visitors were still out. Rex found a waiter who hastened to fetch brandy. Martin took Sally's wrist and in professional manner felt for her pulse. She opened her eyes and moaned:

'Oh ... Martin...'

'Be quiet,' he said. 'Not a word now, please.'

'But you don't understand...'

Then suddenly he bent over her and spoke in a savage undertone:

'You little fool, Sally. *I do know.* I do know, *everything!*'

Sally stared blindly up at him, then shut her eyes and passed from an instant of dazed horror into complete unconsciousness from which she did not awaken for a long time.

This time when she came back to her senses she found herself lying on her bed. She was alone with Martin. He sat beside her and was moistening her lips with cognac.

She stared up, her face and brow damp, her hair dishevelled.

'Oh!' she sobbed under her breath. '*Oh!*'

'Keep quiet,' said Martin, and it was not an unkind voice, but rather the calm authoritative tone of the practising physician.

'But … Rex … what have you said … what has *he* said…'

'I'll tell you later. You're to keep quiet now.'

'Where is he?'

'Do you want him?'

'No. *No!*' she panted, and hid her face in her hands.

Martin looked at the bowed fair head. Naked pain contorted his face, a pain which she did not see.

'Trencham has gone. I sent him away.'

Confused and still struggling against mists that threatened to fog her brain, Sally sank back on the pillow and began to sob hysterically.

Martin took her hand.

'Stop that, Sally. Stop it at once!'

That name, her own name from his lips sounded so odd, so incredible, that it helped to restore her to some composure, as nothing else could have done. She conquered the desire to laugh and cry together and lay still, breathing hard and fast. Unconsciously her fingers were clinging with desperate strength to his hand, clinging until they almost hurt. She thought in the dark recess of her confused mind:

'Everything's finished. It's all over now. All over … and I've failed Martin … and Phil … and myself!'

For a while neither of them spoke. Sally lay there with shut eyes, battling with herself, and Martin looked at her with something of a fatalistic expression on his thin face.

He, too, realised that 'it was all over'. The fences were down. There was no further need for pretence on either side. But the whole thing imbued him with a sense of horror. He could see no light on the horizon. They were all in a dark morass, a whirlpool from which they could not well escape. He shrank from the thought of the pain, the bitterness, the humiliation which must be their lot whether innocent or guilty.

At length, Sally opened her eyes, gave him a long look and then loosened her fingers from his clasp. She lay like a dead thing, white and supine. She said:

'How long have you known?'

He answered:

'I knew ... that night.'

'Why didn't you tell me?'

'I nearly did dozens of times, and then I decided to find out more. Obviously I couldn't understand *then*...'

'But how did you know ... who I was...?'

He got up and taking his sticks, limped painfully away from her bed, poured himself out a glass of water from the carafe over the basin, and drank it. His throat was parched. He said:

'I went to your room that next morning and found a letter in your bag. A letter from *Phil.*'

Sally drew the back of her hand across her eyes in a dazed fashion.

So he had known since *then*. How incredible! For the first time in their relationship together she resented something that he had done. She resented acutely the fact that he had found out and kept it from her. Just as a punishment, of course. He had wanted to torture her. How well he had succeeded! And how easy it was now for her to understand so many changes in his demeanour.

'Oh God!' she said in a voice of agony. 'Oh God, what a mess it is!'

'You're right,' he said. 'It's a bloody mess,

for which you and Phil are responsible.'

'I know – I admit it,' she whispered.

'It was a pretty plan,' he said. 'A unique and original performance, and it almost worked, my dear. Almost, but not quite. I think you'll also admit that it was the most unpardonable thing that either of you could have done. It's had devastating results that have probably destroyed the whole lot of us.'

Sally wished that she could die before he had spoken those words to her. She said:

'I probably deserve a lot of condemnation, but I beg you not to say too much to me just now. I just can't stand it.'

He lifted his brows and looked at her almost with humour on his face.

'No? Well, I suppose the strain has been considerable. In fact, I am surprised that you carried it off for as long as you did and as well. Hadn't you better tell me everything?'

His bitter sarcasm made her wince, but she said wearily:

'What do you want to know?'

'Everything. You see, I'm in the dark about so much of this delightful affair. I know nothing beyond what my wife wrote to you from Etoile-sur-Mer. I didn't, of course, realise that *you* had a fiancé on the scene.'

'Naturally not. Will you please tell me what's happened to – to Rex?'

'He drove away from here half an hour ago.'

'What, in heaven's name, does he think?'

'Nothing, except that you've decided to break your engagement. The poor devil knew nothing about your masquerading in my wife's place, so I saw no object in telling him. The less people in the world know about it, the better for us all. It wouldn't be an attractive scandal.'

The shamed blood seemed to scorch her whole body.

How he despised her! He must think she was the lowest thing on earth. This was the hour that she had waited for and dreaded ever since her love for him had begun to spring in her heart. This was the punishment which she had known must follow wrong-doing. But, while she accepted it, she suffered more than she had thought it possible for any human being to suffer. For what could be worse than to be regarded with scorn and horror by the man for whom you would willingly die? She whispered:

'I agree that ... it wasn't necessary for Rex to know and much better not. Thank you for ... not enlightening him.'

'I didn't do it for your sake. I did it more for my own and perhaps his. The fellow seemed dejected about losing you but at least he retains some pleasant memory of you which he wouldn't have done if I'd informed him that you'd been living as my wife for the last few weeks.'

Sally could no longer lie there while his withering scorn was heaped upon her. She sat up, swung her legs over the side of the bed, and with trembling hands began to do up the little satin blouse which he had unfastened when she fainted. She said:

'What did you tell Rex?'

'That you were my wife's secretary and that he had probably spoken to a new servant at the house who knew nothing about it, and that my wife was also here in the hotel. I went so far as to say that we knew that you had decided to break your engagement, and advised him to let things alone for the moment and get into touch with you later. To which he answered that if you really felt that way he'd just as soon never see you again, and that I was to tell you that there were as good fish in the sea as ever came out of it. That,' added Martin, 'seemed to me a trifle vulgar, but I've repeated to you exactly what he said.'

Sally nodded. So Rex had gone for good. That was something to be thankful for; he had gone and Martin had not given her away. That saved a lot of trouble. But there was plenty left. Martin spoke again:

'Do you mind telling me where my wife is at this moment?'

'I really don't know, except that she must be on the sea now. She was coming back from Spain via Gibraltar.'

285

'And she is with Ivor Lexon?'

'Yes.' Sally could not trust herself to look at Martin. Her cheeks were burning, her throat hurting.

'And you aided and abetted...'

'No, no!' And now Sally swung round and faced him, her head flung back and her eyes blazing. 'I didn't do that. I never dreamed that Phil wanted to get away for *that!* You've got to believe me. You've got to ... why that letter that you read ... that must have shown you that I didn't know...'

Some of the frightful bitterness seemed to fade from Martin's soul. Yes, he remembered that now and was glad. Curiously glad to find an excuse anywhere for this girl.

'That is so,' he said. 'I suppose Phil took you in just as she did me. Whatever happened between us, you know, I never thought that Phil was unfaithful.'

'If you only knew how much I wanted to spare you from ever knowing.'

Martin felt weak and tired. He moved on his sticks to an armchair beside the window and sat down heavily and lit a cigarette.

'I can't quite credit any of it. It seems to me so incredible and so monstrous ... the whole affair! As for me, I must be all kinds of an idiot to have allowed you to get away with it for so long. But the likeness between you two is astounding. No two women have a right to be so alike ... it's fantastic-' He

286

broke off and flicked a burnt match with an angry gesture into the waste-paper basket. Then he took a long, almost sullen look at the girl who was still sitting on the edge of the bed in a dejected attitude.

'I didn't want this to happen,' she was saying, and kept repeating: 'I didn't want this to happen.'

'For God's sake,' said Martin. 'Did you expect to be successful with such an affair? It was rotten and despicable and could only end disastrously. Surely you could have seen that.'

'You don't understand!' Sally almost wailed the words.

'You're right. I don't. To begin with, what prompted the whole arrangement?'

'There's so much to explain. It's so difficult and I don't suppose you'll believe me but I...'

'Never mind that,' he interrupted. 'It doesn't matter what I believe. I'm prepared to believe anything after this. I can still look at you and think that you're Phil. Perhaps I'm not me. Perhaps *I'm* somebody else!' He laughed shortly. 'God, what a riot this would be for the papers if it ever became public.'

Sally looked at him with an expression of acute distress.

'I'll tell you everything if only you'll accept my word. I know I've lied and that it must look as though I'm simply incapable of the truth because I've done nothing but deceive you, but I swear on my most sacred oath, that I'm not going to lie to you now.'

'Very well. Go ahead.'

So she told him everything. He listened, watching her as though his piercing gaze would get to the very bottom of her mind and make quite sure that this *was* the truth. And somehow he had to believe her although so much had happened to make him wary, suspicious, incredulous.

It all seemed so simple once the explanation was given. Sally had called at the Harley Street house to see her cousin. She found Phil half crazy with irritation and boredom, loathing every minute that she spent with her sick husband, and anxious to get away with her lover. That was the Phil whom he had adored and wanted to go on adoring long after she had disappointed him. That was the woman in whom he had placed his trust and whom now he knew was utterly untrustworthy, untrue. *That* hurt ... the stinging thought of his dishonour at her hands. The humiliation of thinking that she should prefer a man like Lexon to himself. But the actual loss of Philippa's love, of Phil herself, did not seem to matter. It was as though the side of him which had loved and believed in her had died long ago.

Easy to see what followed. Phil was too fond of her comforts, her good times as Mrs

Martin Frome, to wish for a divorce. Lexon had no money. So she had hit upon that infamous plan of putting Sally in her place while she danced off to the Continent with her lover.

They were so marvellously alike. It had seemed a wonderful idea especially, as Sally told Martin, she, personally, had nothing to do and was lonely and hard up. But it was not for any mercenary motive that she had fallen in with that plan. She implored him to believe that. She told him how repeatedly she had rejected Philippa's offer, then finally Phil had threatened to run away and ruin her life and his and had almost hypnotised Sally into believing that she would be doing something noble if she consented to the masquerade and gave Phil a chance to get away and enjoy life. But, of course, Phil had assured her that she was going to friends in Paris and that it was to be a perfectly innocent escapade. Not until that horrible woman, Toni Armnouth gave away the secret, had Sally guessed about Lexon.

The story tumbled hotly and breathlessly from Sally's lips now. And with every word she was making an impassioned appeal to Martin to believe her. She told him how, when she had gone down to his room for the first time and seen him lying there, trying to get on top of his misfortunes, and still so helpless and alone, she had wanted to help.

How when he had accepted her as his wife and she had seemed to comfort him by her kindliness, she had told herself that she could not be wrong to agree to the plan.

Of course, she assured him, she knew now that she had made a fatal mistake, that no motive, no matter how good, justified the proceedings. Future events had proved that. But, of course, it had been too late to regret it once Phil had departed and refused to return.

'Then you began to get better and to tell me that it was I who had helped you,' continued Sally, 'and that helped me to justify my actions again. I did help, oh, I did, didn't I?' she added piteously, like a child who seeks a loophole of escape before judgment is passed.

A slow flush mounted to Martin's forehead.

'Yes,' he said. 'I admit that you did. But what was the use? It would have been better really to let me die.'

That brought a choked exclamation from her.

'Oh, no, please!'

He looked at her with vague wonder. She was so obviously upset and miserable. And why? Only because she had been found out, or was she really just a little fool who had done this thing lightly without realising the havoc it would cause?

'Go on with your story,' he said.

She told him of the difficulties that had arisen one by one, and of her telephone call to Paris trying to recall Philippa.

'I assure you I was bitterly indignant when I learned that Phil was with Ivor Lexon and I didn't wish to go on. But, you see, she had already gone from Paris down to the South of France. Then everything seemed lost and I began to see what a disastrous plan it had been. But my one wish has been to try to carry it off so that you would never know. I swear that, although I suppose you don't find it easy to accept my word.'

Martin gave her a long, deep look.

'I think if you lie to me now you'll be beyond forgiveness. I'll believe you. Go ahead.'

'There's nothing else to tell. I think you know it all.'

'And Phil refused to come back, did she?'

'Yes. She was mad, of course.'

'Bad is the word,' he said, his eyes dark and bitter. 'I would have found it easy to forgive her if she had told me openly about Lexon. But she's been a moral coward. She wanted to break all the Commandments and cover her tracks and keep her position as my wife. That's what makes me feel that I never want to see Phil again in this life.'

'I would never, never have done this, knowing those circumstances,' said Sally.

'You were crazy to do it, anyhow.'

'Yes.'

'And you were engaged to be married. Good Lord, didn't you think of the fellow at all?'

'I didn't think it would matter because Rex would never know.'

'You took a risk on that.'

'Yes. Which only proves to me I was never really in love with Rex.'

He pitched his cigarette end into the empty grate and fixed her with his tired, bitter gaze. He could well believe that she had never been in love with that fellow to whom he had talked down in the lounge an hour ago. A truculent, unattractive man with nothing much to commend him, although Martin imagined that he would be quite a decent fellow in his own fashion. But somehow he could not visualise Sally's exquisite body in the arms of the big, red-faced Rex. No! A pang of sheer pain shot through Martin as he dwelt upon the mere idea of Sally in the arms of any man. Only too vivid were the memories of her in *his* and of those sweet, mad hours in which she had been so utterly one with him, and he had felt that life could offer him nothing more worth while, though he lived a thousand years.

That was the cause of his most deep and secret hurt. That love which she had roused in him. It made him brutal with her now. He said:

'You haven't told me yet why you bothered to be *quite* so kind ... since according to you there was nothing to be gained by it and Phil had told you to treat me with that charming unconcern at which she was so brilliant.'

He saw the blood sweep Sally's face. Her slender hands flew up to hide those burning blushes. Her voice came brokenly through the lattice-work of her fingers.

'Forget that, please.'

'Not possible, my dear. One doesn't forget that sort of thing. And you must remember that it was then that I discovered...'

'I know!' she broke in. 'But I don't want you to remember it.'

His hand gripped both his sticks so fiercely that the knuckles showed white.

'You damned little fool... I tell you these things aren't forgotten. It was the worst thing you did. It isn't a kindness ... just to play with a man's emotions.'

That made her gasp and look at him with stricken eyes.

'I wasn't ... playing ... oh, my God!'

He limped to the bedside and stood before her, looking down at her under lowered brows. His whole body was shaking.

'Then why did you do it?'

'Leave me alone, please.'

'Tell me. Tell me!' he said. 'Don't you see that I could almost kill you for it? Don't you see that you woke something in me that was dead and had much better stayed dead?'

'I didn't think of anything except...'

'Except what?'

She looked up at him mutely. Her face was almost ivory white now. She looked drained of vitality, bloodless as though he had been torturing her, and this was the final execution. The answer was wrung from her:

'If you must know, it was *because I loved you*. I began to love you almost as soon as I took Phil's place... I've loved you all the way along.'

He stood rigid, staring down at her. And he knew that whatever other lies she had told him, this was the truth. The tears were pouring down her cheeks now. She sobbed:

'You must hate me. I won't even ask you to forgive me. But I wish I had died before I hurt you. Oh, please, please go away and leave me alone!'

And then to her amazement he dropped the sticks, sat beside her, put both arms around her and leaned his face against her breast. He said:

'Oh Sally, Sally, I don't hate you. That's the whole trouble. That's why it's so bitter for me. You see, Sally, I love you too. Phil doesn't matter any more. She never was what I imagined. But you've become my ideal of her. And I don't want anything, anybody any more except *you!*'

The wonder of it dried her very tears. Breathless and silent she sat there feeling the warmth of his face against her breast, feeling the clasp of his arms about her. And she looked down at his bent dark head and held her breath in case this miracle should not be true. For it had not seemed possible to her that Martin could love her after what she had done. She had taken it for granted that he would turn from her once he knew the truth.

So quiet did she sit that he heard nothing but the beating of her heart under his cheek. And at last he raised his head and looked at her. Her face seemed to him like the transfigured face of some lovely saint in a stained glass window. And it was strange and wonderful to him in that hour that he did not blame her for anything or feel that she had done wrong. She *was* a saint to be adored.

Then she spoke:

'No, no, it can't be true!'

'What can't be true?'

'That you love me.'

'But I do, Sally. That has been the bitterness of it. I was in love with Phil for a long time but she killed something in me. You brought that something back to life and brought back my ideal of her. And then it ceased to be *her* and became *you!* It's all mixed up inside me, this love. It can't be analysed or understood. It's just there, one and the same love.'

'But I did a terribly wrong thing.'

'Yes, you were crazy. It was an awful thing to do. But I love you!'

She burst out crying again.

'And I love you. Martin, Martin, *Martin!*'

He held her close with a fierce and almost protective gesture and covered her face and her hair with kisses.

'Don't cry like that, Sally darling! Don't!'

'I've hurt you. I've been frightfully wicked. Oh, I know it!'

'I can't remember anything but that you love me. And if you really loved me all the way along, that excuses so much. There's so little real love in the world, my precious Sally, that it's worth holding on to and I'm not going to let this go now. No, I swear I'm not!'

Her arms were about him, hugging him like a panic-stricken child. She sobbed:

'I'll have to go away. I'll have to leave you. I can't stay with you now.'

'I'm not going to let you leave me, Sally.'

'But there's Phil!' she said in an anguished voice.

He released her and sat apart from her for a moment, staring at the floor.

'I know there's Phil. But she can't expect

to stay with me after this. I won't take her back. I don't see why I should! She doesn't care a damn about me and never has done and what she has just been doing is monstrous!'

Sally put the back of her hand against her quivering lips and looked at him with her swollen eyes.

'I've been just as … monstrous.'

'You were in the beginning, perhaps. But I believe you carried on with it out of love for me, and I'm not going to call *you* to account. It's Phil who must pay.'

'You mustn't … divorce her.'

'Why not?'

'Oh, poor Phil…'

Martin laughed.

'It's funny to hear you sitting there, pitying her. What pity does she deserve? She went off with her lover. She had no pity for me. Her only fear was of being poor. Well, I'm rich enough to provide for her as well as for you and me. I don't want to be vindictive. I shan't fling her out and tell her to go to Lexon without a penny. I'll settle something on her. But I'm going to marry you, Sally, and that's the end of it.'

She stared at him.

She had anticipated many kinds of end to the masquerade, but never this! She could not believe it possible. She said:

'You can't want to marry me. Oh, it can't

happen. I'm going away and Phil's coming back.'

'No. I shall never see Phil again.'

'I don't understand,' whispered Sally, and felt her head swimming. 'I don't understand why you should be like this, why you shouldn't hate me.'

'I've tried to explain. I *did* try and hate you when I first found out the truth. I felt bitter and cruel. I wanted to hurt you. I tried to torture you. But I couldn't stop loving you. And when you looked at me just now and told me that you loved me, I believed you, and that's all that matters.'

'God knows it's true that I love you, Martin. I couldn't bear it that afternoon when you found me with that hateful man, Major Frankham.'

'I'd almost forgotten him.'

'But you don't think now that I wanted him to make love to me? I was in a frightful position and...'

'Don't bother to tell me. I suppose it was just another episode of Phil's.'

'He was a cad ... a beast! He had letters from her and he was threatening to send them to you.'

Martin looked at her, a quick warm look.

'That's what mattered to you ... trying to keep the ugly facts from me! Ah, Sally, you've been very wonderful to me and that's why I find it so easy to forgive you, my dear!'

'Wouldn't it be better for you to try and forgive Phil?'

'And let you go? I do believe you would be glad of that if you thought it was best for me. But no, there's only one thing that I want, and that is to keep you with me for ever. Oh, Sally!'

Then she was in his arms again and for a long while neither of them spoke. At length Sally said:

'What are we going to do?'

'That,' said Martin, 'is what we've got to decide.'

17

Sally walked down to the lounge.

She was dressed for dinner. Martin was not quite ready but was going to join her in a few moments. She was almost glad to be alone. When she was with Martin she was so overpowered by the wonder and amazement of this love for her to which he had just confessed, that she could not think straight. All the time she was listening to him, feeling his arms about her, she was in blind ecstasy, loving him from the very depths of her soul. Away from him she was able to see things more impersonally. And she had to think about Phil.

Somehow, in spite of all Phil's infidelities, her callous treatment of Martin and her utter disregard for anybody but herself, Sally was still conscience-stricken about her cousin. Phil had left her here as a kind of 'deputy' and relied on her to keep the secret. She, Sally, had failed. Not willingly, not consciously. But circumstances had altered and swept the matter out of her hands. And now Phil was not coming back to find things just the same, having enjoyed a month's freedom. She would return to disaster, disgrace, divorce. Martin said that he did not hate her. He did not wish to be vindictive. Indeed, he intended to be magnanimous and ease the financial situation for her and Lexon. But he would not contemplate taking her back, even for the sake of his reputation and his work. His profession had always meant a great deal to him, but he told Sally that his love for her came first.

Yet Sally was unhappy. She had been forgiven, but forgiveness weighed heavily on her soul. She was finding it hard to justify herself for what she had done. Even the splendour and astonishment of finding that Martin loved her could not entirely wipe out that sense of guilt.

She was half inclined to run away from him and from everything. An inclination which vanished the moment she was in Martin's presence and she heard him telling her that he could not do without her and that she must never leave him again.

There was so much to think about and to decide, he had said. The tangle was too difficult to unravel in a moment.

While she had dressed this evening Sally had kept telling herself that she wanted to do what was best for Martin, but this time it must be the right thing. She could not break all the laws of convention and society again and be at peace with her own soul.

The fates, however, were taking this problem out of the hands of Sally and Martin and solving it for them. Even while they had been talking things over, while Sally was torn in two by her doubts and her love, the finger of Destiny had moved and written. And the last thing that had ever entered either Sally's or Martin's head was to imagine that death would solve the difficulty. *Phil's death.*

Quite casually, Sally lifted up the evening paper which she found in the lounge and glanced at it while she was waiting for Martin.

Only half interested, she looked down the column and saw a small paragraph headed:

'UNKNOWN ENGLISH TOURISTS FATALLY INJURED IN A SPANISH TAXI.'

The paragraph stated briefly that on the preceding night, a taxi in Malaga, which was a fashionable watering place in the south of Spain, had come into collision with one of the buses which carried passengers into outlying districts. The car had turned over and then burst into flames. So swift and fierce was the conflagration that it had been impossible to get the wretched victims out of the car immediately, although the driver was not as seriously injured as his passengers, and had been able to tell the police that his fares were an English couple who had just arrived from Madrid. They had told him that they were on their way to Gibraltar where they intended to get a boat for England. He did not know their names. And the luggage which had been piled on the car was totally destroyed by the flames before they were beaten out. The unfortunate couple were charred beyond recognition. The police had little means of discovering their identity. Of the woman's handbag, which doubtless contained her passport, etc., there was nothing left save a metal clasp. But they had salvaged a gold cigarette case belonging to the man in which there were cards bearing the name: 'Mr Ivor Lexon', and the address of a club in Piccadilly.

The British Consul was, apparently, still trying to trace relatives or friends of the unfortunate victims. This was difficult because they had, apparently, come by train from Madrid that same evening and had not booked rooms in any of the hotels under the name of Lexon. It was presumed that the woman travelling with Mr Lexon was his wife. The injured driver had heard them address each other by familiar and affectionate terms.

It was the name 'IVOR LEXON' which leapt out from the newspaper at Sally and held her attention riveted. White as death, she read what that paragraph had to say, and then shut her eyes tightly, feeling terribly sick.

A moment later, still clutching the paper, Sally stumbled into the lift and was taken up to her suite. Trembling from head to foot, she rushed into Martin's room. Martin, who had just finished tying his black tie, turned to her.

'Darling, what is it?'

Dumbly she handed him the paper, and with a shaking finger pointed to the paragraph which held so sinister a meaning. Through dry lips she whispered:

'Lexon … and *Phil* … don't you see? *It must be Phil!*'

Martin scanned the paragraph rapidly. Then he, too, felt sickness overtake him and dropped into a chair. He said:

'Oh, my God!'

'It must be Phil, mustn't it?'

'You say they were going to Spain?'

'Yes. Coming back via Gibraltar. There can be no doubt about it.'

'No, I suppose there can be no doubt.'

'And nothing left … not even her passport … nothing to tell who she is … my God, how *ghastly*.'

Martin held out a hand and pulled Sally down beside him.

'Don't think of it. It doesn't bear thinking about.'

She shook her head dumbly and covered her face with her hands.

'Poor, poor Phil!'

And Martin Frome echoed:

'Poor Phil,' and remembered his wife suddenly not as the callous egotist who had done so much to hurt him, but as the young and charming Philippa whom he had married and loved.

That was the end! The end of her beauty and youth and her desires. She had died before half her life was over, with her lover. The pair of them, exterminated … wiped off the earth!

It was too horrible to contemplate.

Martin looked at Sally who bore so strange, so close a resemblance to Philippa and who was more to him now than she had ever been. He took one of her hands and hid his eyes against it.

'Oh, Sally!' he said.

'There can be no mistake, can there, Martin?'

'I should say none.'

'Ought we to go out there?'

'We will, of course.'

'You're not fit to travel.'

'I shall be all right. We can fly. I have a patient, an American millionaire whose life I saved; he has a private plane and has offered me the use of it at any time that I want it. I don't mind asking him to let us take it.'

'But what can you do when we get there?'

'I don't know. We must think. Does anybody else in the world, except yourself,

305

know that Phil went away with Lexon?'

'Not a soul. She left me here in her place so that the alibi should be perfect.'

Martin took a handkerchief from his pocket and wiped his forehead. The shock had unnerved him, but he made an effort to keep calm. There were so many things to think about, and there had leapt into his mind the sudden realisation that if they managed things carefully enough there need be no scandal, no slur attached to Phil's name. *In fact, nobody need ever know that Phil had died.* There was not a living being who could identify her. No one who could tell the British Consul the real name of Ivor Lexon's travelling companion.

Sally met Martin's gaze. A long look passed between them. Then she whispered:

'What are you thinking, Martin?'

'I'm thinking,' he said, 'that from every point of view, it might be best if Phil remains … unidentified.'

Sally stared.

'It can do no good,' he added, 'for me to go to Malaga and say "This woman was my wife." It would only cause a horrible scandal. So many people at home believe that you are Philippa. Don't you see, Sally, that this thing, ghastly though it is, may be the solution to our whole problem?'

She looked at him, breathlessly.

'We just do … nothing. And *she* and Ivor

306

Lexon are buried together out there, probably as husband and wife?'

'Yes.'

'And I...' Her voice faltered and words failed her.

'You stay for the rest of time – as *my* wife.'

Sally rose to her feet, crossed to the window, and looked out at the autumn night which was dark and starless. She thought suddenly of Philippa as the little cousin who had played with her, and of days when they had taken each other's places and played practical jokes on their parents. Phil, who had been like herself, so uncannily like ... and was now a charred unrecognisable body, to be consigned to a lonely, nameless grave in an alien land. Suddenly with eyes full of scalding tears, Sally turned and looked at Martin. She said:

'It would be the most wonderful thing in the world to stay with you always as your wife, Martin. And I agree that, for all our sakes, it would be best to leave things as they are. But can't we do something ... for her?'

'I have thought of that, too,' Martin nodded. 'I was wondering if I could go out to Malaga and get in touch with the Consul without giving away the whole show.'

'No, you mustn't go. You aren't fit. But I shall go.'

'My dear, what can *you* do?'

'I can say that I knew Ivor Lexon. In a

roundabout fashion I can find out whether there is any possible clue left to identify *her* ... and if not, I shall just say that out of friendliness for my countrywoman...' Sally's voice broke '...I would like to pay for her grave ... for a stone...'

Martin put his face in his hands, a grey, tired face, which looked suddenly old. The whole thing was so terrible and even with Sally left ... lovely, living Sally, he was haunted by the dead Philippa.

Sally crossed the room, stood before him and stroked his head gently.

'Let me go Martin. Let me go out and do what I can.'

'Very well,' he said, 'but you'll come back to me, won't you?'

'If you want me to.'

He put his arms around her and pressed his head against her breast. She felt him shuddering.

'I need you now more than ever.'

The tears dripped down her cheeks.

'I still don't know why you've forgiven me so easily. I still feel so guilty. I've been so much to blame...'

'Forget that, Sally. We must both forget it. It won't do for us to remember anything now, except that we love and need each other.'

She leaned down and kissed his hair.

'Do you think anybody will ever find out?'

'I don't think it's possible. Trencham

assured me that he didn't intend to get into touch with you again. You have no relations, no friends who might try to find *you*, I suppose?'

'Nobody. My father's death left me quite alone in the world.'

'And poor Phil had no relatives alive, except odd cousins who have never been in intimate touch with us; and our friends, most of whom have accepted you.'

Sally shut her eyes tightly.

'But I don't see how ... how it's possible for you and I...'

'We must marry, of course,' he broke in, guessing her unspoken question. 'I'm determined upon that. It's the only way in which we can go on living together. Sally, if nothing else happens during the next few weeks, I see clearly what we must do.'

'Yes?'

'We must go away, right away from everybody who has known us. I don't think we could either of us stay in London, where you would have to go on being *Phil*. It would make us both nervy and wretched, and we would never be really happy. We must begin again – somewhere else.'

'Oh, but Martin ... your precious work...'

'I can carry that on wherever I go. Just before my accident, I was in touch with a specialist from Sydney and he besought me to go out there one day. He said they'd need

309

of a man like myself. Could you bear Australia, Sally? It's the other side of the world. But, no doubt, it has its compensations and I could practise there if I wanted to.'

Sally drew a deep breath.

'Going to the other side of the world with you wouldn't hold any terrors for me, Martin. But I feel it would mean so much to you to leave your hospitals and your London friends.'

'I should miss Cheniston and Stenning, perhaps. But there are hospitals in Sydney and new friends to be made, a new practice to build up. And if you were with me as my wife, oh, Sally, I do believe I could be happier than I have ever been in London, with poor Phil.'

'That's all that I want,' she said. 'All that I have ever wanted ... for you to be happy.'

Martin raised his head and looked at her. Her face was wet with tears, passionate and yet maternal. And in her eyes was the expression which he had always loved in the eyes of that woman in the painting with the curly-headed child in her arms. His heart gave a great warm leap. The grey horror of Phil's death seemed to fade a little. He clasped Sally's warm young body closer to him and said:

'My darling, my darling ... you will be my real wife... When all this is over we shall be happy together – always...'

18

Those words: *'We shall be happy together ... always...'* were to Sally like a shining star in the darkness during those next six weeks when there seemed very little happiness and much sorrow. For there was so much to be gone through before either she or Martin could begin to attain happiness. Yet the hope, the promise of it was always there to relieve the darkest moments and to pull her through what had, necessarily, to be a period of waiting.

Slowly, but surely, the tangle unravelled itself, and the day approached when Sally was able to forget that she had ever committed the mad folly of masquerading in another woman's place, and to lose all sense of guilt and feel that from all time she had been destined to walk at Martin's side, knowing unquestionably that it was her rightful place.

Twenty-four hours after they had read the report of that car accident in Spain, Sally left Martin to try and get what benefit he could from the rest and change in Devonshire, and went out to Malaga.

Under her own name, Sara Browning, she

travelled, first by air to Paris, then train to Madrid, and yet another train down South.

Her interview with the British Consul was of some importance to her, because it left no possible doubt in her mind that it was indubitably Philippa who had perished in the accident. Having introduced herself as a 'friend of Ivor Lexon's', Sally was given more details of the catastrophe than the papers had printed. Nobody had claimed relationship with Ivor Lexon and the remains of his travelling companion, believed to be his wife, so Sally was told, had been consigned to the grave with him. A lady's platinum ring set with diamonds, remained as sole evidence to the fact that the poor young woman was married ... at least they presumed that was so because it was the type of ring used for weddings these days. On it was the Inscription: 'P. from I. Forever', and the date, 'Sept. 2nd, 1934'.

Sally was shown this ring and asked if she could throw any light on the matter; whether she knew if Mr Lexon had recently been married.

And Sally looked at the little jewelled circlet lying in the palm of her hand, a piteous trophy, and felt a great lump in her throat which for a moment prevented her from answering any questions. She knew so well what that inscription meant. *P* for *Philippa* ... and that date, *Sept 2nd* ... the date on which Philippa and her lover had crossed to Paris for their 'month's holiday'.

Tragic, illicit honeymoon! Mad folly! And at the end, death in all its grim finality. Poor Phil!

Sally told the Consul that she did not know anything about Ivor Lexon's private affairs and could throw no light upon the matter. But she begged him to accept a sum of money which would provide a suitable stone and pay for the attendance of the grave in that little Spanish cemetery enclosed in high white walls, blazing under the blue of Spanish skies.

Her 'charitable and generous contribution' was gratefully accepted, and she was promised that the grave of the unfortunate and mysterious couple should not be neglected.

No one had come forward to identify the dead woman in spite of all inquiries, so Miss Browning was asked to accept the little ring, since she had so kindly paid for the funeral expenses.

Sally returned to England and handed the ring to Martin, who was back again in Harley Street. It seemed to him tragic proof of his wife's death.

And after that Martin and Sally separated again. By mutual wish they decided not to live under the same roof until they were married, and that marriage could not take place in England where so many difficulties would attend the procuring of the licence. It was agreed that Martin should be the first to go to Australia, and that Sally would follow when he was ready for her there.

It was a shock to Harley Street when Martin Frome put his house up for sale and handed his practice over to a junior at the hospital. But it was taken for granted that his recent accident and illness had made it difficult for him to work again and when he went to Australia it was presumed that it was a journey in quest of health, rather than a voluntary exile.

A month later when a society paper reported that *'The beautiful Mrs Martin Frome had sailed for Sydney where she intended to join her husband,'* there was little comment and only the usual amount of idle gossip among Philippa's acquaintances.

Toni Arnmouth maintained that 'Phil had gone off in a huff because Lexon had been graceless enough to die in the company of the woman who had supplanted her.'

Philip Frankham, who had never had the courage to blackmail Phil and send those letters to her husband, came to the conclusion that he had better give up his pursuit of Phil. She had changed altogether too much for his liking. Besides Australia was a damn long way off and mutual friends of the Fromes said that they intended to settle out there.

Of the chosen friends, Jan and Dacre Cheniston were genuinely distressed at the loss of Martin. But they agreed that what he had done was a good thing for him. He had seemed anxious to get away, and his wife, whom they had thought at first extra-ordinary inconsiderate to let him travel alone, had called to say good-bye to them the night before she, herself, sailed for Australia, and almost convinced them that she was anxious to be with Martin and make a new home for him.

This was a conviction which strengthened as the months went by, and the letters they received from Martin were of the happiest.

He liked Sydney, he said, and there was much that he found to like in the Australians. He had bought a most attractive house which looked over the loveliest harbour in the world, and he was already absorbed in new work, having been warmly welcomed by the medical profession in Sydney.

His health was excellent. He was walking well, with only one stick, and Phil (that was the name by which the Chenistons must always know her) was marvellously fit. They had never been more content.

'Thank God for that,' Dacre Cheniston said to his wife in the English spring after one of Martin's enthusiastic letters. 'I do believe the old boy has got what he wanted out of life at last.'

'And I know something else,' said Jan, her dark eyes smiling at her husband. 'His dearest wishes are going to be satisfied. You remember how he adored our babe and how we always thought he ought to have a child of his own. Well, I've had a letter from Phil and she says there's a baby due in the autumn. What do you think of that?'

'I think it's grand,' said Dacre. 'I'm terribly pleased.'

But, of course, there was so much that the Chenistons did not know, and which could never be conveyed to them by either Martin or Sally, who had started that new and wonderful life together in their Australian home.

They could never know, for instance, of that marvellous morning when Sally had landed at Sydney and Martin had met her, looking browner and fitter than she had ever seen him, and they had been gloriously re-united. That morning when Sally had been married to Martin by special licence and could sign her name as 'Sally Frome,' and feel that at last she belonged to the man whose name she had once taken against all laws.

Besides, whatever they might write to their friends in England, neither Martin nor Sally could ever express the real depth of the happiness and contentment which was theirs. But they could express it to each other and were never tired of doing so.

The day came, as Martin had prophesied, when they were able to forget all past tragedies, forget even that Philippa Frome had existed, and remember only that they lived for each other.

They had brought nothing with them from England which could possibly remind either of them of the days when Philippa and Martin had lived together. Martin had disposed even of the oil painting of Philippa's mother which had once given him so much pleasure – and so much bitterness.

But there was a living picture for him to look at now, and one of which he would never grow weary.

The picture of Sally and his son; that son who was born to them in the golden spring of the Australian year. Martin knew whenever he looked at them that he was more than ever in love with Sally, the wife, and that he worshipped Sally, the mother.

Once she asked him:

'Do you ever regret coming here ... do you ever miss London and the old life?'

And he answered:

'This is the only life I have ever known. In England I never lived at all. I only existed. You and the boy and our home mean love, life, everything! Are you happy, too, Sally? Do *you* ever regret?'

And she with one arm about him and the

other about her son, gave a low laugh of pure contentment and whispered:

'Don't I look happy?'

'You look very beautiful,' he said and kissed her and the baby in her arms.

The publishers hope that this book has given you enjoyable reading. Large Print Books are especially designed to be as easy to see and hold as possible. If you wish a complete list of our books please ask at your local library or write directly to:

Dales Large Print Books
Magna House, Long Preston,
Skipton, North Yorkshire.
BD23 4ND